THE SAGA OF QUEST INC.

THE APOCALYPSE

LYNN MATHAI

authorHOUSE®

AuthorHouse™ LLC
1663 Liberty Drive
Bloomington, IN 47403
www.authorhouse.com
Phone: 1-800-839-8640

Published by AuthorHouse 09/18/2014

ISBN: 978-1-4969-4032-2 (sc)
ISBN: 978-1-4969-4031-5 (e)

Library of Congress Control Number: 2014916462

In loving memory of
my grandparents
and
Uncle Pete

With love to my parents and my sister.
For my nephews and niece,
Lynn Papa loves you three always;
you are his heart and everything.
To Luca C. (SM), Mr. Becker, and Jenna,
thanks for all your help.
To everyone at AuthorHouse,
especially Ella Centino, thank you.
And last but not least,
to all you readers
who joined Phil and the members of Quest Inc.,
thank *you*.

Dakota

Lynn Mathieu

PROLOGUE

Muggsy lit the torch and entered the dark, damp, dusty corridor, followed by Phil, Alex, and the other members of Quest Inc. The corridor led to an enormous cavern.

"The information that was given to me says that the Philosopher Stone is in this cavern," Muggsy said loudly. "And the half of the map we have shows that as well."

"Now what?" Alex asked.

"We dig."

Muggsy threw each of the Q.I. members a shovel, and they started to dig. The ground slowly began to crumble away and then got increasingly faster. They all fell into the dark air. Just before hitting the ground, they stopped inches away with a jolt.

"I'm glad we harnessed ourselves to the wall up there," Muggsy exclaimed.

There in front of them was a small wooden box on top of a stone and sand pillar.

"Yo, Phil, I think we should *tag team* this!" Alex said.

"Whatever you think," Phil replied.

"What do you mean, 'tag team' it?" Muggsy asked.

"You'll see."

Phil and Alex went and stood at either side of the pillar. Phil opened the wooden box, and Alex raised a diamond in the air. The stone shone brightly. Just then, there was a faint whistling sound. Alex looked down to see blood on his Q.I. suit. Everyone looked and saw two arrows lodged in Alex's stomach and lower chest. He blinked his eyes and fell to the ground.

"Crap, this hurts like hell."

CHAPTER 1

The Return

It was a warm spring day in May, and the streets of New York City were hustling and bustling with students and businesspeople. A young man and woman around the age of seventeen walked out of the NYU apartments. They were both holding suitcases and a box in their hands. The young man closed the door behind him, and they slowly made their way down into the subway and got on the F train, pulling in their suitcases just as the doors were closing. For a while, the subway car was quiet, until music from an iPod filled the air and people began talking.

An hour later, the young man and woman got off the train at the Union Turnpike stop and transferred to the E train. As soon as they entered the train, they heard the talking, music, and laughter that filled the air. Moments later, the train door opened and a plump man came into the subway car and sat next to them. The man, one of their college professors, leaned over and began to talk with them. Fifteen minutes later, they said good-bye to their professor and left the train. They slowly climbed the stairs and made their way up to street level. When the Q43 bus came, they boarded, swiped their metro cards, and sat in the back.

After another hour passed, the bus arrived at their stop, so they got off and started walking. Five minutes later, they stopped in front of the Glance of Angels Orphanage. They smiled at each other and made their way up the walkway. Reaching the front door, they pressed the doorbell. Seconds later, the doorknob turned and the door opened. Doris, the orphanage cook, was standing in the doorway smiling at the young man and woman. She hugged them, and the three of them went to the den and sat down.

"Hi, Phil and Calista. How are you two doing?" Doris asked. "We haven't seen you in four months."

"We really missed being here," Phil replied. "And we missed your home cooking."

"Then why didn't you visit for spring break?" Doris asked.

"You know how it is. It just feels uncomfortable being here ever since Alex died," Phil replied.

"How do you think we feel? We all feel the same way," Doris said as tears rolled down her face. "We all cared about him."

"How's Muggsy doing?" Phil asked.

"She's not taking it very well; she started smoking cigars and cigarettes again," Doris began to explain. "And she's been coming home late from hanging out with Toby."

"And Lisa?" Phil asked.

"She's still trying to get over Alex's death, but she's doing better," Doris said. "Go get washed up; lunch is almost ready."

Phil and Calista grabbed their bags and went upstairs. Calista kissed Phil on the cheek and walked away. Phil walked into the boys' dorm and put his bags on his bed. As he glanced at Alex's old bed, a tear rolled down his cheek. A second later, he fell to his knees by the bed and broke down crying. Doris came into the boys' dorm; she sat next to Phil and tried to console him.

"We all miss him," Doris said, tears again streaming down her face. "And there's nothing we could have done to save him."

"There is something I could've done!" Phil yelled. "I could've saved him."

Doris wrapped her arms around Phil and held him tightly. "You couldn't have gotten to him in time, and even if you had, there's nothing you could've done to stop him from dying," Doris said sadly. "Destiny and fate are intertwined, and there's nothing we can do to stop them."

"I'm sorry for yelling at you."

"That's okay. Just get changed and come down to get some lunch." Doris kissed Phil on the forehead and slowly left the room.

Phil got up, opened his suitcase, and began unpacking and putting his things away. He then changed his clothes and left the boys' dorm. He made his way quietly to the girls' dorm and knocked on the door. Calista opened the door, and they walked down to the dining room together. They each got a plate of food, and when they were done eating, they went to the kitchen, put the plates into the sink, and went upstairs to the boys' dorm. The whole house was so quiet that you could hear a pin drop.

Suddenly, the front door opened and footsteps running up the stairs echoed throughout the orphanage. The footsteps echoed even louder when they reached the second-floor landing. A second later, Isaiah and Brandon came into the boys' dorm. Isaiah and Brandon saw Phil and Calista and smiled; they walked over to them both.

"Oh my gosh, we missed you," Brandon said.

"How is everything?" asked Isaiah.

"Everything's okay," Phil replied. "How's everything with you guys?"

"We are doing all right; we are doing pretty well in school," Isaiah said. "The two of us, as well as Madison, are graduating in two weeks."

"I'm really sorry that they had to hold you back a year," Phil said quietly. "How's the tutor I set you up with?"

"Lisa has taught the three of us a lot. She should be home from college in about two hours," Isaiah said.

A few moments later, Madison, Stanchie, and Melissa came into the room and hugged Phil and Calista. They all held hands and sat down.

"We missed you so much," Madison said excitedly.

"Hey, Phil, Calista told us that you got a job in the NYU library as a digital media technician," Melissa said. "They must really like you to give you a job like that your freshman year."

"It's a good job, and it's pretty exciting," Phil said as he turned toward Brandon and Isaiah. "We heard that you two and Madison are the new junior commanders of Q.I."

"Well, somebody had to take over and be junior commanders when you suddenly left Quest Inc.," Brandon said softly.

They continued to talk for about an hour. Afterward, Madison, Brandon, Stanchie, Isaiah, and Melissa left the dorm, leaving Calista and Phil alone. Calista leaned over and whispered something into Phil's ear and then got up and left the room. Phil took a pair of swimming trunks out of his dresser and changed into them. He then went to the girls' dorm, where he met with Calista. She was wearing a red-and-white-striped swimsuit. They held each other's hands and went downstairs and out to the backyard; the yard was strangely quiet.

A gentle breeze was blowing through the warm spring air. They got into the pool and began swimming and playing around in the water. After a while, they climbed out of the pool and sat down on two lawn chairs. They eventually got up and went inside. When they reached the second-floor landing, Phil went to the boys' dorm and changed into his dry clothes.

Phil sat alone in the dorm just thinking. He realized that the reason he was around people all the time was to fill the emptiness inside him. His parents had left him in death when he was a young child, when he was only three years old. There was a void in his heart from not being hugged or kissed by his parents, and he filled this void with many good friends.

A lot had happened to Phil these past two years. His last remaining living relative, his grandpa Buzz, had passed away, leaving him a large amount of money. His grandfather had also left him a legacy of the secret organization Quest Inc. Phil's grandfather had created Quest Inc. to help in certain difficult situations. The only way to gain access to the Quest Inc. headquarters was through a secret lift in the main office; access was only permitted to Quest Inc. members.

Like Phil, most of his friends in the orphanage had lost their parents and loved ones. And like Phil, his friends in the orphanage were members of the secret group, Quest Inc.

Alex, his lifelong best friend, had died due to complications from a bad injury months after the last Q.I. mission he was on.

Phil went to the computer desk; he turned on his work laptop and sat down. He put a USB memory stick into the laptop, opened up the NYU website, and began to edit it.

Moments later, there was a loud knock at the door, and he called, "Come in." Lisa walked into the room and went over to hug Phil. She pulled up a chair and sat next to Phil.

"Hey, Phil, how is everything? What are you up to?"

"I'm doing well. My supervisor asked me to reformat and edit the NYU website. How is Adelphi University treating you?"

"My course advisor put me into advanced classes, and it's pretty fun tutoring Isaiah, Brandon, and Madison."

"Thanks for tutoring them for me. How are you?"

"I'm doing okay, I guess." As Lisa replied, her voice cracked and tears began rolling down her face. Lisa and Phil held each other and started to cry. A couple of minutes later, they broke apart and wiped the tears off their faces.

"I have to go tutor them now. I'll talk to you later, Phil."

"Okay, I'll see you at dinner."

Lisa left the dorm, and Phil continued to work on the website.

A little while later, Phil picked up his head. He realized he'd been sleeping at the computer desk. Everything seemed fuzzy and unusual. He got up from the chair and collapsed onto the floor. His legs felt numb, and he was queasy. The room and everything around him seemed really far way. He carefully made his way to the second-floor landing and went downstairs to the dining room. The atmosphere of the orphanage was strangely eerie and quiet, and the dining room felt creepy. He walked into the kitchen, grabbed a glass out of the cabinet, and filled it with ice-cold water. He'd just begun drinking the water when he suddenly dropped the glass, shattering it.

Alex was standing in front of him in the shadows as he slowly walked into the light. Alex's eyes were a pale gray, and he had black drooping bags under his eyes. The skin on his body was drooping and peeling away, and there were bald patches where his hair had been. He let out a loud and long groan.

"Phil, please help me from my eternal damnation. Only you and Quest Inc. can help," Alex said, letting out another long groan. Alex reached out for Phil with his long bony fingers, and they stared into each other's eyes. At that moment, Phil jolted awake.

It was only a dream—a bad nightmare—but it had felt so real. Noises and voices from the other kids echoed through the house and filled the air. He saved his work to the memory stick and then put the laptop away. He tiredly looked at the clock. *It's only seven o'clock,* he thought sadly.

He went downstairs to the dining room and got a plate. He dished up his food, sat down, and began eating. Lisa, Calista, Isaiah, Madison, and Brandon soon joined him, and they began talking. As Phil was eating, he was staring into the air with a blank look on his face. Brandon asked Phil a question, but Phil just continued to stare blankly.

He felt so alone, as if nobody knew how he felt. But how could anyone know how he felt? So many bad things had happened to him in the past two years. Phil got up from the table and went to the kitchen to put his dishes in the sink. He slowly returned to the boys' dorm, and lying on his bed, he began to cry. A couple of minutes later, he heard kids in the hallway, so he wiped the tears from his face. A group of boys came into the room and sat around Phil, starting to talk to him. A little while later, the boys said good night to Phil and left the room. Moments later, Calista came and gave him a kiss good night before returning to the girls' dorm. Phil crawled into his bed, pulled the covers over himself, and fell asleep.

Around one o'clock in the morning, the door of the dorm slowly swung open and someone came into the room and walked over to Phil's bed. The person gently shook Phil. He pulled the sheets off his face, blinked, and stared at the person with a blank look on his face. The person moved out of the shadows and into the moonlight; it was Muggsy, who is in charge of the orphanage. Muggsy looked the same, although there was a slight gray streak in her hair. The aroma of cigars and alcohol were heavy on her clothes and breath.

"How is everything, Phil? I missed you so much."

"Everything's okay, and I've missed you too. I see you broke your promise and are still drinking and smoking."

"Right now it's very hard to keep that promise I made to you. Besides, I have no motivation to quit when I want to die myself."

"You know what your motivation is? Me. Me and all the other kids you promised to take care of."

Tears rolled down her cheeks as Muggsy began to cry. Phil held her tightly and tried to console her.

"If you don't want me to be your motivation, fine, but don't quit on those children that are still here. And do it for Quest Inc."

Muggsy wiped her face dry and softly smiled at Phil. "Do you realize that Q.I. hasn't had a mission since Alex passed away?"

"You must be kidding me," he said. "Well, is Quest Inc. still getting sponsored?"

"Yes, it is, and the money you gave us is really helping too. We're just not getting any missions. Go back to sleep. We'll talk in the morning."

As Muggsy left the dorm, Phil threw the sheet over his head and went back to sleep.

CHAPTER 2

The Ooze

In the morning, the sunlight broke through the closed blinds and slowly filled the orphanage. Muggsy walked into the boys' dorm and opened the shades, allowing light to pour through the room. The other boys jumped out of their beds and began hustling and bustling around the room, but Phil merely yawned and stretched. He got out of his bed and left the dorm. He went to the dining room, got a plate of food, and went to a table to eat. When he was done eating, he quickly left the dining room and made his way to Muggsy's office. He knocked on the door.

"Come in," she called.

Phil went into the office and sat down.

"Phil, guess what. We have a Quest Inc. mission," said Muggsy.

"What? Who's it for?"

"Well, you remember the strange earthquake that we had three day ago. Even though it was a small one, it made a crack in front of Our Lady of the Snows Church. So the monsignor called me and asked if we can take a look at the crack because there's something oozing out of it."

"Do you have any idea what it could be?"

"I have no idea, but it's probably nothing."

"When are we going to do this thing?"

"As soon as Ryan comes and gets his gear," replied Muggsy.

"Just let me know when he comes. I'll be in the game room."

Phil went upstairs and made his way to the game room. The room was empty; it seemed desolate, as if it hadn't been used in months. He slowly looked around the game room and remembered the last time he and Alex hung out together. He went over to the pool table, racked up the pool balls, selected a pool cue, and started playing by himself. A couple of minutes later, the door to the game room swung open and Ryan walked into the room. Ryan's usual straight hair was now puffy and shaggy, and he looked slightly older than the last time Phil had seen him. Ryan had dark bags under his eyes as if he hadn't slept for days, and he was wearing the Quest Inc. suit.

"Are you coming with us?" Ryan asked. "We're leaving now."

They left the game room and went downstairs to Muggsy's office.

"Hey, Phil, are you going to suit up?"

"No, Muggsy. I don't feel comfortable being in it right now. Who's coming with us?"

"Nobody. Just the three of us are going."

Muggsy got the keys to the Hummer, and they left the orphanage. When they got into the Hummer, Phil looked in the trunk, where he saw radios and other equipment. Muggsy put the key in the ignition and started it up. The Hummer quickly pulled out of the driveway and sped down the street.

The Hummer wove down the street between moving cars, and a couple of minutes later, they reached Our Lady of the Snows Church and parked in front. As they got out of the vehicle, the monsignor greeted them. Ryan got the equipment from the trunk, and they followed the monsignor. He led them to the crack, and they began to set up the equipment. Ryan pointed to a test tube and a tool that looked like a pencil. Phil handed them over to him. A little later, Ryan stopped working and went over to the monsignor.

"There are no signs of radiation or other harmful materials, but there's one more test I want to run," Ryan said.

Ryan walked away, and a couple of minutes later, he returned with equipment that Phil had never ever seen. It was a Sony UX microcomputer connected to a Sony P series computer, with a liquid measurer, test tube, and a microscanner attached to it. Ryan turned it on and set it up. He then scooped some of the ooze out of the crack and put it into the test tube. It began to scan the ooze, and a couple of minutes later, it started to beep and words appeared on the screen.

"It found small traces of ectoplasm residue and genetic residue in the ooze. But it's probably nothing," Ryan said.

"What do you mean by ectoplasm residue?" Phil asked.

"It means spiritual after matter," the monsignor said.

"There's only a tiny trace of it, so I don't think you have anything to worry about," Ryan said. "Do you mind if I take a sample of this for further testing?"

"Of course you can," the monsignor said.

As Ryan began scraping ooze into a test tube, the monsignor took Phil aside.

"Hey, Phil, you haven't come and spoken to me in a while," the monsignor said. "Do you want to talk to me about anything?"

"Not really—at least not now," Phil replied.

"I know that you've had a hard time, but if you want to talk to me, I'm here for you," the monsignor said.

"I heard that you're becoming a bishop. Congratulations," Phil said.

"Yes, thank you."

The monsignor bid them farewell and left. Once they'd loaded the equipment back into the trunk, they drove back to the orphanage and went to Muggsy's office. Muggsy punched in the code on the keypad, and the lift rose. Once the three of them got on the lift it slowly began to descend. A couple of minutes later, they arrived at the Q.I. headquarters. Other than the new flat-panel big-screen computers, everything in the headquarters looked pretty much the same. Ryan took the ooze-filled test tube out of his pocket, put it into a hemoglobin divider, and turned it on. It slowly began to spin around and gained more and more speed.

The three of them heard a loud booming sound from the lift descending again, and a few seconds later, Calista, Isaiah, Madison, and Brandon entered the headquarters. Madison ran over to Phil, wrapped her arms around him, and gave him a bear hug.

"Oh my gosh, Phil, I missed you," Madison said.

"I missed you too, Madison. How are you?"

"I am doing fine. A lot of things have changed while you have been gone."

"Why haven't we seen Ruth since we've been back?" Phil asked.

"She joined a coven," Muggsy called out.

Phil and Calista looked at each other smiled and laughed.

"I kinda figured she would," Calista said.

Moments later, everybody left the headquarters, leaving Ryan and Muggsy alone.

Late that afternoon, a strange thing happened. Phil felt a slight breeze in the room and saw Ruth standing in the doorway. She was wearing a long black gown and black high- heeled boots that went up to her knees. Phil quickly stood up, and they hugged each other.

"How is everything? I have not seen you since you came back home," Ruth said.

"Everything's good. I heard you joined a coven," Phil said.

"Well, I am doing it to improve my sorcery skills, but I am still a part of Quest Inc.," Ruth replied. "Guess what! I got a job at Joe's Pizzeria as a tavern maiden."

"That's awesome!" Phil said happily. "And I think people would like it better if you called it pizza server. Are you doing anything right now?"

"Not really."

"Would you like to come to the cemetery with Lisa, Calista, and me?"

"Of course I will come with you."

"I just have to change and get the girls; I'll meet you in the living room."

Phil changed into a black button-down shirt and black pants. Seconds later, he left the room, went to the girls' dorm, and knocked on the door. Lisa and Calista went with him to Muggsy's office. The office door was open, so Phil peeked in. Muggsy was sitting at her desk, crying silently. Seeing Phil looking at her, she wiped the tears from her face.

"Come in, come in. You can come in," Muggsy quickly said.

"Are you okay?" he asked.

She merely sniffed and nodded.

"Can I borrow the keys to the Hummer?" Phil asked as they entered. "We want to go to the cemetery."

"Of course you can," Muggsy said, and she suddenly began crying again.

"Muggsy, would you like to come with us?" Phil asked.

"Yes, I would like that," Muggsy replied.

They met Ruth in the living room and left the orphanage. They got into the Hummer and drove away.

The vehicle sped along the roads, and Muggsy stopped at a small flower shop before they arrived in front of the main gates of Flushing Cemetery. They went inside, made a quick right, and walked straight for five minutes. Finally, they reached a small headstone that read:

ALEX FUKDOSKI
MAY 15, 1996 – MAY 15, 2012
FRIEND TO ALL AND LOVED BY EVERYONE

They knelt down in front of the tombstone, placed the flowers in front of it, and began to cry. Just then, a breeze blew through the air and circled around their faces. A while later, they got up and left the grave.

"Phil, did you know I haven't been here since you left for college?" Muggsy said.

"Why haven't you?"

"Guilt and fear, I guess. I just can't handle the thought of being here alone."

"In many ways, I feel the same way," Phil answered. As they walked out of the cemetery's main gate, Phil had an eerie feeling.

When they got back to the orphanage, Lisa and Calista came into the boys' dorm and they began talking.

The phone ring, and shortly after that, Muggsy came into the room. "I'm going out with Toby," she said. I'm putting Doris and the three of you in charge. Just keep an eye out on the younger kids." Muggsy left the room, leaving the three of them alone again.

"Ever since you two left, Muggsy has been going out to who knows where with Toby," Lisa said.

A bunch of the kids came into the dorm room to hang out with Calista, Phil, and Lisa. At seven o'clock, they all went downstairs to the dining room for dinner. When Phil and Calista were done eating, they went up to the game room and began to play pool. Madison and Isaiah came and joined them in the game. At around nine thirty, the telephone rang. A few minutes later, Doris ran into the game room.

"Do you mind watching the kids for me?" Doris quickly asked. "I'll be right back."

"Okay, we will," Calista replied. "But what happened?"

"I got a call from Toby to come pick Muggsy up," Doris replied.

"No, I'll go pick her up. Where is she?" asked Phil.

"Oh my gosh, Phil, thank you so much. She's at Dillon's Pool Hall," answered Doris.

Phil went downstairs to Muggsy's office, grabbed the keys off the hook, and left the house. He quickly jumped into the Hummer, started it up, and drove away. When he got to the pool hall, he went inside and found Muggsy sitting down in the far corner of the large room; she was looking quite sick. Toby, Muggsy's best friend since childhood, walked up to him.

"It's nice to see you, my boy, after so long," Toby said.

"You too," Phil replied. "What happened to her?"

"She had a little too much to drink and got into a fight; she also broke a pool table," Toby said.

15

Just then, the pool hall owner walked up to Toby and Phil. "Who the hell is going to pay for the damages?" the woman asked.

"Give me a week, please. I promise I'll come and pay you for the damages," Phil replied.

"Shut up, you fat cow!" Muggsy yelled at the owner.

"Shut up right now, Muggsy!" Phil shouted back.

The pool hall owner began to walk over to Muggsy, but Phil stopped her.

"Please don't. I'll take care of this," Phil begged.

"I'm going to come after her if I don't get my money in a week," the woman said.

Phil and Toby went over to Muggsy and carried her out of the building on their shoulders. They put her in the back seat.

"Thank you so much for calling us about Muggsy. We really do appreciate it," Phil said.

"You're welcome, and I would've done it anytime," Toby replied.

Phil got into the Hummer and drove off; when he got back home, he helped Muggsy inside to the office and helped her lie down on the office couch.

"You'd better think about what the hell happened tonight," Phil said angrily.

Phil went upstairs to the dorm and threw himself onto his bed. All night he was tossing and turning in his bed, nearly waking up the other boys. In the morning, sunlight flooded the whole orphanage, waking everybody up, and they all went down for breakfast.

As the day drew on, the orphanage was strangely quiet; usually the house was filled with footsteps and laughter. For most of the day, Phil worked on the NYU website, and that night he hung out at the orphanage with his friends.

The days slowly passed, and the nights were warm and breezy. The weekend was hot, almost sweltering, and the kids spent the entire weekend inside the house enjoying the cooling breeze of the air-conditioning.

The hot spring weekend finally ended, and the house was still oddly quiet. As the week slowly drew on, the air outside began to cool down. The kids started playing outside again, and Phil started hanging out at the park again.

Isaiah, Madison, and Brandon's graduation was drawing closer, and they began preparing for it. Phil helped the teens with their speeches, and Muggsy began food shopping for the graduation pool party.

The morning of the graduation, everybody got up and started to get ready for breakfast. When the kids were done eating, they began to get dressed for the graduation. After they got ready, they went down to the living room, where Muggsy and Doris joined them to get pictures. A half hour later, Toby arrived, and they all left the orphanage. The kids piled into both the Hummer and Toby's Range Rover. When they got to Martin Van Buren High School, Isaiah, Madison, and Brandon went to join the other graduating students, and Muggsy, Toby, Doris, and the other kids went to the auditorium.

When the ceremony started, the guest speaker got up and approached the podium. Twenty minutes later, Mr. Goldfine, the principal, walked up onto the podium and began to clear his throat.

"Congratulations to the graduating class of twenty thirteen," Mr. Goldfine started to say. Everybody applauded. "Three students have shown more than exemplary work and study ethics. These are the class's graduating valedictorians: Isaiah Mathais, Madison Pullorkunnel, and Brandon Pullorkunnel."

Everybody began to clap again, and Muggsy and Phil started to whistle and cheer. As the three of them walked up to the podium, Doris and Muggsy took pictures. Isaiah took out a piece of paper and prepared to begin reading their speech.

"Good morning, teachers, visitors, graduating students, and all of you here at the twenty thirteen graduation of Martin Van Buren High School," Isaiah began. "At times, we thought we would not make it, but we did."

Madison spoke next. "With a lot of hard work and determination, we all did it." "We are entering a new phase in life, the next step in being young adults."

Next it was Brandon's turn. "We want to thank Mrs. Martin and our other teachers, our friend Lisa for tutoring us, other friends for helping in their own way, and Muggsy and Doris for letting us stay with them."

"And finally, to the graduating class of twenty thirteen, keep working hard and keep shooting for the stars," Madison, Isaiah, and Brandon said at the same time.

As they left the podium and walked off the stage, everyone began to stand up, clap, and cheer. A little while later, Mr. Goldfine began giving out the diplomas to the graduates, inching closer and closer to Isaiah, Madison, and Brandon. Finally, it was their turn, and as they got onto the stage again, everybody began clapping and whistling. As Mr. Goldfine handed them their diplomas, Muggsy and Doris smiled and took more pictures.

"I present to you the graduates of the class of twenty thirteen!" Mr. Goldfine called out.

Phil had been looking over the many faces of the twenty thirteen graduates, and he suddenly spotted a familiar face. It was Alex. Their eyes met, and the pale face of Alex seemed to stare at him intently with glowing eyes. Phil gasped and looked away. What was going on? Alex had died, so how could he be here in front of him?

The students threw their caps in the air and cheered. Phil searched for Alex in all the chaos, but he had disappeared. A second later, the graduates slowly lined up and marched out of the auditorium, with everyone following them. When everybody got into the main hallway, Muggsy and Doris took pictures of Isaiah, Brandon, and Madison with their friends. The main hallway slowly began to empty out until no one was left.

"Lisa and Calista are going to take the new graduates to the park; can you help me set up the party?" Muggsy asked Phil.

"Okay, but can we make a quick stop?" answered Phil in a dazed state.

"Okay, where?" Muggsy asked.

"Dillon's Pool Hall," Phil replied as he regained his composure.

"Why do you need to go there?" Muggsy quickly said.

"Well, somebody has to pay for your stupidity at the pool hall," Phil replied.

Muggsy stared at Phil with a sad look on her face.

They didn't speak to each other for the rest of the ride, and when they got to the pool hall, Muggsy parked in front and Phil got out of the Hummer. A couple of minutes later, Phil got back into the Hummer, and both vehicles were soon back at the orphanage. Phil went out to the backyard and began putting up the CONGRATULATIONS and HAPPY GRADUATION banners. Toby set the plates, cups, and napkins on the table. Doris began setting up the barbecue grill and Muggsy set up the turntables and other DJ equipment.

The kids arrived back at the orphanage to get ready for the party. A little while later Ryan, Matt, Zack, and some of the other kids' friends came over. Muggsy led them to the backyard. The kids from the orphanage started coming out to the backyard, so Muggsy began working the turntables and playing music.

"The food will be ready in a little bit. Relax and have a good time!" Muggsy said into the microphone.

Phil, Calista, and Lisa sat down at the edge of the pool, and the other kids got into the pool. A little while later, the guests of honor—Madison, Isaiah, and Brandon—got out of the pool and started talking with their friends. The music and the aroma of the foods filled the spring evening air, and the kids began dancing.

"The food's ready, everybody, so come get some grub and keep this party pumping and jumping," Muggsy called out.

The kids grabbed plates and cups and got their food and sodas. Phil got a plate of grilled mushrooms and a veggie burger. He went and sat with Lisa and Calista again, and they began eating.

"I'm going to get something to drink. Do you want something?" Phil asked.

"I'll take a Coke," Lisa replied.

"And I'll have the same," Calista said.

Phil went to the table and opened the ice-filled cooler. He got cans of Coke for the girls and a Mountain Dew for himself. When Phil got back to his seat, he saw Brandon, Isaiah, and Madison sitting next to them talking. Phil handed Calista and Lisa their sodas and joined in the conversation.

The evening drew on, growing darker and darker by the minute. The kids got into the pool and began playing water volleyball, boys versus girls. When the game ended an hour later, the girls' team had won. The music continued to fill the air, and the kids slowly got out of the pool and began dancing again. Phil and Calista started slow dancing with each other. The graduates' friends eventually began to leave, and the party slowly died down. Lisa, Phil, and Calista helped Muggsy clean up. When they were done, Phil took the leftover food to the kitchen and put it in the refrigerator before heading to bed.

CHAPTER 3

The Possessed

Summer had finally arrived; the following morning was a wave of heat. Phil slowly got out of bed, yawned, and looked around. He was the only boy left in the room. When he was done getting ready, he went down to the dining room and ate breakfast. He then went to the game room, where Isaiah and Brandon joined him and asked if he wanted to play pool. Ten minutes later, Muggsy came into the room, got a cue, and joined in the game. When the telephone rang, Muggsy left the room. Her voice faded as her footsteps went down the stairs.

An hour later, the boys left the room, and Phil went to the boys' dorm and worked on the NYU website. When he was all done editing the site, he saved the changes to the memory stick and took it out. He put the memory stick on top of his dresser and left the room again. He went to the backyard, sat down at the edge of the pool, and started thinking. Thoughts of his grandfather and Alex swirled through his head. Lisa and Calista eventually came outside to the pool. Phil took off his shirt, slowly got into the pool, and started swimming. Isaiah, Madison, and Brandon joined the group, Isaiah and Brandon jumping into the water.

After they'd had enough swimming, they dried themselves off and went back inside. Once in his dorm room, Phil changed out of his wet swim trunks, throwing them into the hamper, and then he took the memory stick from his dresser and left the room again. He went downstairs to Muggsy's office and knocked on the door. She told him to come in, so he opened the door, went inside, and sat down.

"I need to go to my boss's house and give him this memory stick, and I was wondering if I could use the Hummer," Phil said.

"First of all, you can't borrow the Hummer to go there," Muggsy started to say, "and second, I'm not letting you go there by yourself. So either I come with you or you don't go at all."

"This is so unfair. Why can't I borrow the Hummer … and why can't I go by myself?"

"You just got your license and are still learning—that's why. I also don't want you to go by yourself because I don't know what is in his mind," Muggsy replied.

"You don't have to worry, but you do what you have to do," Phil said.

"I'll meet you in the living room in five minutes," Muggsy said.

Phil quickly went to the living room and put on his shoes. As he was tying his sneakers, he noticed that there was a little dirt on them, so he took a tissue and began cleaning them.

Lisa walked into the room and started to laugh. "Stop trying to make your sneakers look *GQ*," she said. "Where are you going, anyway?"

"I have to go give this memory stick to my boss," Phil replied.

"Okay, I'll see you later." She turned and left the room.

When Muggsy pulled up in front of Phil's boss's house, they walked up the long driveway and finally reached the ranch-style house. The windows looked old and the shutters even older. Although the house was old, the front door looked brand new. Phil pressed the doorbell, and a few seconds later, the door slowly swung open. Phil's boss, Jeremy, was tall and rather skinny; he had a long mustache that led into a goatee. He was wearing a long lime-green robe over a pair of black pajamas.

Jeremy was an eccentric kind of guy. He came off as a rich well-cultured man of the world. He liked to think that he would have had a successful future, but his fate would not be so kind to him.

"Hey, Phil, how are you?" his boss asked.

"Everything's just fine, Jeremy. I just wanted to give you the work I did for the NYU website," Phil said. He took the memory stick out of his pocket and handed it to Jeremy.

"Wow, that was quick; I thought that would take longer. I'll submit this when I go to work this afternoon." Jeremy slowly looked over at Muggsy "You must be Muggsy. Phil's told me a lot about you. It's nice to finally meet the beautiful face behind the name."

Muggsy looked at Jeremy, smiled, and laughed. "Thank you, but I don't know anything about you. Phil really hasn't mentioned you," Muggsy said.

"Maybe we can talk over dinner sometime," Jeremy said.

"Okay, that would be nice," Muggsy replied.

After leaving Phil's house, they stopped by McDonald's and got lunch for everybody at the orphanage. They returned to find everybody heading to the dining room. Phil and Muggsy ran into the dining room and put the bags of food on the table.

"Where's Doris?" Muggsy asked the kids.

"She's in the kitchen warming up lunch," one of the girls said.

Muggsy hurried into the kitchen and stopped Doris just as she was about to warm up the food. "Don't warm anything up; I bought everybody food from McDonald's," Muggsy said.

"And you couldn't call me and let me know this?" Doris asked with irritation.

When Phil was done eating and had changed his clothes, he met Lisa, Isaiah, Stanchie, Madison, Brandon, Calista, and Melissa in the den. They went to the park to play some basketball. Twenty minutes later, Zack and Matt arrived, and they and Phil started to shred on their skateboards. A while later, the boys began playing handball while the girls sat down by the fence and watched them. As the afternoon ended and it grew darker, the park began to empty. The boys got their skateboards and headed back.

When they got to Matt and Zack's house, the two boys kissed Melissa and Stanchie, said good night, and went inside. When the others returned to the orphanage, Phil went to the boys' dorm. Muggsy came into the room a little while later and sat next to Phil.

"Are you coming down for dinner?"

"No, I'm not really hungry right now."

"Are you sure? Doris could make you a veggie burger."

"Yes, Muggsy, I'm positive I'm not hungry. I'm just going to go to sleep."

"Okay, I'll see you in the morning."

Muggsy got up, turned off the lights, and left the room. Phil slowly climbed into his bed and went to sleep.

In the morning, when Phil went down to the dining room for breakfast, he saw that nobody had turned on the lights because the bright sunlight was breaking through the shades and brightening the house. Right after he ate breakfast, Phil went to the backyard and began shooting hoops. Suddenly, dark clouds rolled in, the sky turned a grayish black, and it started lightning and thundering. A loud clap of thunder rumbled through the sky, and a lightning bolt hit the neighbors' TV antenna. Phil went back inside and closed the door, certain it was going to rain.

Calista walked over to him, and he asked her if she'd heard about any thunderstorm today.

"No, not really," Calista replied. "And you know the strange thing? As soon as the thunder and lightning started, the TV and radio went out."

Phil and Calista went up to the boys' dorm. Some of the younger boys were scared and in their beds. Phil turned on the MP3 radio and tuned it to the 10.10 WINS news.

"An unexpected lightning and thunderstorm has occurred in New York," the news person started to say. "I repeat: an unexpected lightning and thunderstorm has occurred in New York."

Phil and Calista went over to the younger boys and began calming them down.

Meanwhile, at Flushing Cemetery, the sky was a darker grayish black than anywhere in New York. The thunder clapped even louder than before, and bolts of lightning began hitting all the tombstones. The muddy ground of the cemetery began shaking, and the tombstones began cracking. A deep endless hole etched itself in the ground and a shapeless demon rose out of the hole. The shapeless figure growled, snarled, and slowly looked around at the graves. The figure's eyes darted and stared at one particular tombstone. It felt such pain and anguish coming from the tomb. It quickly glided over to the tomb and broke through it; the tomb began to splinter and collapsed into pieces.

The ground began to shake even harder, and the grave imploded and then blew up. A hand shot out of the rubble of the grave, and the decaying corpse slowly dug itself out of the ground. The skin of the decaying corpse started to rejuvenate, and an evil smirk came over his chapped lips. Another shapeless figure rose out of the hole and slowly looked around. Jeremy, Phil's boss, was visiting his mother's grave, and just as he was leaving, he turned around and saw what was happening. He had never seen such a horrifying sight in his life.

He ran as fast as he could toward the main gates. The figure quickly glided closer and closer toward Jeremy. Suddenly, something seemed to be creeping up his leg, and then his stomach, until it took over his whole body. Jeremy fell to the ground screaming and crying in agony, violently rolling around on the ground. Jeremy slowly stood up from the ground with an evil smirk on his face and his eyes glowing. But this was not Jeremy, as something had wiped away his conscious mind.

Back at the orphanage, Muggsy and the Quest Inc. members went to Muggsy's office, and they all headed down to the Quest Inc. headquarters. Everyone sat down, but Muggsy remained standing. Just as she was about to talk, the ooze in the test tube started bubbling over and the test tube exploded. The ooze continued to bubble, and then it formed itself into a hand and began clawing at everybody. Muggsy quickly snatched a garbage can and threw it over the ooze. She then sat on the garbage can.

"What the hell was that, Ryan?" Muggsy asked loudly. "You said it was just ooze and that nothing's wrong with it."

"I was clearly wrong. This is bad," Ryan replied.

"Well right now, we have to contain this thing," Muggsy called out.

"We could put it into the cryogenic containment unit," Ryan answered. Ryan ran over to a far corner of the room and opened a freezer, removing a tank-looking object from it. He punched a code into a keypad, and the tank slightly split apart. A second later, it automatically opened wide. There was steam slowly bellowing out of it from the frozen liquid nitrogen. Ryan put the ooze into a large test tube and quickly covered it. Then he grabbed it with tongs and placed the test tube into the liquid nitrogen. Ryan punched in the code again, and the cryogenic unit closed. Muggsy put the unit back into the freezer.

"I'm sorry, everybody, but the meeting is postponed until further notice," Muggsy said. "I have to find out what's going on."

Everybody but Muggsy and Ryan filed out of the headquarters.

Meanwhile at the cemetery, the two demons who had taken possession of the two bodies broke into an old run-down house and began murmuring to each other. They were looking for a mirror. The first demon screamed in horror when he saw his physical body. He found that he possessed Alex's dead body. The demon looked the same as Alex, but his skin was whiter and his eyes were dark yellow.

"I possessed the body of a young fleshling!" the demon in Alex's body exclaimed. "The body of a stupid young fleshling. But no matter—this can prove useful to me. Supay, does my father know of our plans?"

"No, Azazelbog, Satan doesn't know of our activities or plans," the second demon replied. Then he looked in the mirror as well and saw that he looked like Jeremy.

"My father and God can fight for the peoples' souls, but this world shall be my new playground and my new home," Azazelbog exclaimed loudly. "Now let us feed."

The storm slowly abated, and the stars in the night sky shined like glitter. Inside the orphanage, the kids were hanging out in the dorms and the game room. A while later, Muggsy called the kids for dinner. When Phil was done eating, he went back to the dorm and hung out with Isaiah and Brandon. Minutes later, Lisa, Calista, and Madison showed up.

"Did we tell you the good news?" Isaiah asked.

"No, what is it?" Phil asked.

"Isaiah, Madison, and I have received full scholarships to Adelphi University," Brandon replied.

"Oh my gosh, that is really good news," Phil said.

"Yes, it is! Hey, do you guys wanna go to the game room?" Calista asked.

"I'm really sorry to be a killjoy, but I'm not in the mood to hang out, I just want to go to sleep," Phil said.

"Okay, then we'll see you in the morning," Lisa said.

Calista kissed Phil before they all left the room. Phil climbed into bed and fell sleep instantly.

The following morning after breakfast, Phil went up to the girls' dorm and hung out with Lisa and Calista. The morning air outside was warm, but the sky was still cloudy; they heard birds chirping through the opened window.

Meanwhile in the cemetery, there were pools of blood leading up to the old run-down house, and inside it, Azazelbog and Supay were feeding on twenty peoples' bodies. When they were done feasting, they wiped the blood off their faces and smiled.

"That feast was quite satisfying," Azazelbog said as he smirked. "I haven't feasted on fleshling flesh in five hundred years."

"The brains of young fleshlings taste especially good," Supay added. "But what if Satan finds out what we're doing?"

"He won't. He's too busy with his own war with God. Besides, by the time he finds out, this world will be my new home and the fleshlings will be my own cattle."

"I'm sorry for upsetting you lord Azazelbog," Supay said.

"Come, let's look for fleshling followers. And when they have out lived their use, we may feast on them," Azazelbog said.

Azazelbog and Supay left the house and looked around the graveyard for people. Ten minutes later, three goth teenagers came into the cemetery. Supay and Azazelbog jeered at each other and walked over to the teens. Azazelbog stared into their eyes as though looking into their souls.

"Tell me your deepest, darkest secrets and desires," Azazelbog said as he read their souls. "Ah, you have some darkness in your hearts."

Then Azazelbog turned to the third teenager, looked into his soul, and saw that he was good. "You will join me, you goody-goody, or you will die," Azazelbog said.

"I don't know who you are, so I don't want anything to do with you," the boy replied.

"You have chosen your fate, and now you will suffer for it. Say hi to my father in hell for me," Azazelbog softly said.

The boy screamed and cried in agony as he combusted into flames. His screams echoed through the air as his flaming body turned into ashes and blew away. The other two teens screamed and ran in fear. Azazelbog's and Supay's wings unfolded, and they flew after the teens. Just as the teens reached the main entrance, Azazelbog and Supay appeared in front of them and snatched them by their necks, flying back to the house. The door blew open so hard that it fell off its hinges. Azazelbog and Supay threw the teens into the corner of the room, where they fell to the ground with a loud thud. They came down to the floor, walked over to the teens, and pinned them to the wall by their feet.

"You two have two choices: be my followers or die and join your friend in hell," Azazelbog said, "Hey you never know—my father might make you his new pets."

When the two teens started screaming for help, Azazelbog moved his hand across their mouths; their mouths suddenly disappeared.

"Now make your decision," Azazelbog said.

He moved his hand over the teens' faces again, and their mouths reappeared.

"We will never join you!" one of the teens yelled, and they began screaming for help again.

"I don't like that answer, so I'll make your mind up for you," Azazelbog softly said. Azazelbog stared into their eyes, and the teens looked as though they were in a hypnotic trance. A second later, the teens dropped down to the floor on their knees and bowed down to Azazelbog and Supay.

"How may we serve you, masters?" the teens asked simultaneously.

"Ah, that's what I like hearing—filthy fleshlings obeying us," Azazelbog said.

The demons looked at each other and began chuckling. Supay's tongue darted in and out, tasting the air.

"I smell fleshlings in the graveyard, my lord," Supay said to Azazelbog.

"Go find those fleshlings so we can feast," Azazelbog said to the teens.

"Yes, our lord," the teens replied.

The two teens left the house, and Azazelbog and Supay smirked at each other.

At the orphanage, Phil, Lisa, and Calista were talking in the boys' dorm room, and Isaiah, Brandon, and Madison soon joined them. The six of them decided to go out to the pool. After they swam for a while, Phil made his way up to the boys' dorm and changed into dry clothes. He then headed down to Muggsy's office. The office door was open, so Phil went inside. Muggsy was sitting at her desk listening to Notorious B.I.G. He sat down in a seat and got her attention.

"Muggsy, do you mind if I go to the cemetery?" Phil asked.

"Of course I don't mind. Do you want me to come with you?" Muggsy asked.

"There's no need for that," Phil replied. He left the room and stopped to say hi to Lisa and Calista in the living room.

"What are you doing?" Calista asked.

"I'm going to go to the cemetery," Phil replied. "Do you want to come?"

"Okay, I'll come with you."

Phil and Calista asked if Lisa wanted to go with them.

"No, not right now," Lisa replied. "My heart's just not ready to go there right now."

"Okay, we'll see you later," Calista said.

Phil and Calista made their way to the bus stop and waited. When the bus finally came, they got on and sat in the back. After about thirty minutes, the bus stopped at the cemetery. When they got out, Phil noted that the beautiful night sky was filled with twinkling stars and it was strangely cold. When they got to Alex's tomb, they gasped in surprise to find a long wide crack in the headstone and the grave imploded, with dirt scattered everywhere. Then they heard a low chanting that got louder and louder by the second; it seemed to be coming from the catacombs. They slowly walked over to the catacombs and went deeper and deeper into them, heading into a large cavern with empty tombs in the walls.

The two teens from earlier were in the corner of the cavern, and there were about twenty people with them. Suddenly, Azazelbog and Supay emerged from the shadows. Phil's and Calista's mouths dropped open, and their eyes darted toward Azazelbog. Thoughts raced through Phil's head. Alex was supposed to be in a coffin eight feet under the ground. How was it that he was standing right in front of them? And why did he look so demented? And the other guy looked like his boss, Jeremy. What had happened here? Phil was so confused.

"I can read your thoughts, boy!" Azazelbog called out to Phil. "Bring the fleshlings over to me," Azazelbog told the two teens.

The teens and two of the followers grabbed Phil and Calista by the shoulders and dragged them to Azazelbog.

"I know of your family, and it is well that I do," Azazelbog whispered into Phil's ear. "Have you ever wondered why lord Keals and Michael Gittman were so evil? Their hearts were not always evil. They sold their souls to my father and me, and in doing so, their hearts and souls became evil, withered things, growing even more evil through the years."

"Who the hell are you … and why do you look like Alex?" Phil yelled.

"How dare you speak to lord Azazelbog!" Supay snarled. "You stupid little fleshling."

"Don't silence him just yet, Supay. He should know the answers he seeks before they both die. We possessed these bodies so we could go unseen by human eyes and go ahead with our plans to turn this world into our new home. And soon it will be too late to stop us." Azazelbog said to Phil, "I have chosen this body because I felt such pain and regret surging through this body. Now you will die knowing the fate of your world fleshlings." Azazelbog turned around. "Demoo, Cheko, come feast on your dinner."

Phil and Calista whirled around to where Azazelbog and Supay were looking; out came snarling and growling hellhounds. The hellhounds were three times larger than pit bulls but looked similar in appearance. There were enormous sharp jagged spikes penetrating through the hellhounds' spines, and their entire bodies were covered in visible muscles and pumping blood vessels. Their eyes were pitch black, and they started glowing. The hounds snarled even louder. Phil and Calista began running for their lives, and the devil dogs chased after them. Calista and Phil turned the corner and hid behind two huge headstones, and the hounds started sniffing them out.

The hellhounds spotted the two of them, and they snarled again. Phil and Calista sprang to their feet and ran toward the main entrance, the hounds trailing behind them. Just as they got to the main gates, Phil and Calista looked behind them. The large sharp jaws of the hellhounds were about to clamp down on one of

Phil's legs when one of the hounds rose up into the air and flew into a huge headstone. It fell to the ground with a loud thud and started whimpering.

Phil quickly turned to see what had happened. He saw Ruth next to him; she smiled and winked at him. The other hellhound clamped its jaws onto Calista's ankle and began dragging her away. Ruth turned around and started chanting. A huge gust of wind shot out of Ruth's hands and hit the hellhound. The hound let go of Calista's ankle, and it flew into a tree. A group of women walked out of the shadows and surrounded them. Ruth picked Calista up off the ground and hoisted her onto her shoulders. Ruth, Phil, and the group of women ran out of the cemetery.

They ran faster and faster down the street to make it on the bus. Azazelbog swooped down in front of them and folded his wings back up. Azazelbog tried to hypnotize Phil into coming to him, but Ruth blocked the hypnotizing force. Azazelbog punched Ruth in the stomach, dropping Calista onto the ground.

"I know what you really are, even though you are in Alex's body," Ruth said, gasping. "I feel your evil presences all around you."

"And I know who you are, witch," Azazelbog snarled.

Ruth slowly began to chant: "Zeg deebo, delfah him; denhava." A huge surge of energy shot out of Ruth's hands and hit Azazelbog, causing him to fall back.

"Can you walk, Calista?" Ruth asked.

"No, I don't think I can," Calista replied.

The Q88 bus was about to leave, but Phil flagged it down and it came to a halt. The front door of the bus opened, and they all quickly climbed on.

"Go quickly," Ruth said.

"First, you guys have to pay your fare," the bus driver exclaimed. "Second, what the hell happened?"

Ruth was getting ready to explain to the driver when Azazelbog quickly sat up and opened his wings.

"What the hell is that?" the driver screamed. The driver slammed his foot on the gas pedal and the bus sped away, running over Azazelbog. Phil made his way to the back of the bus and looked out the window; Azazelbog was flying behind the bus and slowly caught up to them.

"Let us try to bind him from harming us," Ruth said to the women with her.

The four women stood at the four corners of the bus, with Ruth standing in the dead center, and they started chanting an incantation. A warm calming feeling came over the whole bus and the people on it. A second later, there was a crashing sound on top of the bus and a deep dent appeared in the bus's roof. Azazelbog flew into the sky and came soaring back down, crashing into the bus. Fortunately, everybody jumped out of the bus as it slowed down, for it imploded and the windows blew out.

After the smoke and debris cleared, Ruth cautiously looked out. "Is everybody okay?" she called.

"Yes we are," the people that were on the bus began murmuring.

The bus driver quickly got to his feet and ran away. The remains of the bus began to move; Azazelbog ripped the rest of the bus in half and threw it at them. Ruth stopped the bus and sent it back; the bus half fell on Azazelbog, pinning him against a building. A second later, the bus was set ablaze and turned into ashes.

"You think you can use witchcraft against me?" Azazelbog called out.

"No, but we wanted it to be a challenge for you," Ruth said.

One of Ruth's friends took a dagger out of her cloak and threw it at Azazelbog, piercing him in the chest.

"You think your mortal weapons can destroy me?" Azazelbog asked. He began laughing and slowly pulled the dagger out. The dagger wound began sizzling and boiling. "What did you do?" he demanded.

"We dipped that dagger in holy water," Ruth replied.

"I will be back, and you will be sorry, fleshlings!" Azazelbog screamed.

Phil and Ruth held Calista by the shoulders, and they all walked as quickly as they could the rest of the way to the orphanage. Once there, they helped Calista to Ruth's bedroom and settled her on Ruth's bed. Ruth and Phil began gathering herbs and started crushing them up and mixing them together. When the mixture was ready, Ruth spread the mixture over Calista's wound and chanted a spell. Phil and Ruth left the room, leaving Calista to rest. About an hour later, Ruth and Phil came back and checked on her. Ruth took the sheets off Calista's legs; the wound looked as if it healed well. Just as they were about to leave the room, Muggsy walked in; she stared at Calista and then looked at Phil and Ruth.

"What the hell?" Muggsy asked.

Phil and Ruth took Muggsy aside and explained to her what had happened.

Muggsy walked to Ruth's bed and ran her fingers through Calista's hair. "Don't worry—you'll be just fine," Muggsy said to her. She came back over to Phil and Ruth. "I have to go make a couple of phone calls. I'll come check on her a little later."

Muggsy quickly left the room, and Phil and Ruth sat down next to Calista.

"I just want to go to the girls' dorm and rest," Calista said.

Phil and Ruth helped her off the bed and then assisted her upstairs to the dorm. Calista sat on her bed, and Phil kissed her before leaving the room.

CHAPTER 4

The Vision and the Coven

In the morning, Phil got ready and went to the girls' dorm, but it was empty. He went down to the dining room to eat, but he didn't see Calista. When he was done eating, he left the room and met some kids in the hallway. He asked them where Calista was, and they told him they didn't know, so he went up to the game room. He turned on the PlayStation 3 game console and played Halo 3 and Splinter Cell. Two boys came in the room and racked up the pool balls. They grabbed cues and asked Phil if he wanted to play, so Phil turned off the game console and played pool with them.

As the pool game, which Phil had won, ended, Ruth and Calista came into the room. Calista was walking as if nothing had happened to her; the wound from the hellhound's bite had totally disappeared.

"How is that wound gone so fast?" Phil asked.

"I'm not sure. I think it was the herbal mixture Ruth put on it," Calista replied.

"It was not so much the herbal mixture. It was the healing spell I cast," Ruth said.

"Where were you?" Phil asked.

"I ran to the store and picked up eggs for Doris," replied Calista.

"I have to take care of a couple of things. I'll see you later," Ruth said.

"Where are you going?" asked Calista. "I thought we were going to hang out."

"I wanted to cast some protective spells around the orphanage and the Q.I. headquarters," Ruth replied. "Muggsy and I were talking, and this thing is serious."

"Okay, we'll see you later," Phil said.

A few minutes after Ruth left, Phil and Calista went to the boys' dorm to hang out. Lisa, Brandon, and a group of soon kids joined them. A little later, the doorbell rang and the front door slammed shut. There were whispers and low talking in the living room. The voices became louder as footsteps echoed through the stairwell as people headed upstairs. Moments later, Pat and Lynda walked into the room and hugged Phil and Calista.

"Hello, my pigeons. How are you doing?" Lynda asked Calista and Phil "We haven't seen you since you've come back."

Pat turned to Phil and looked at him, smiling. "How are you doing, my whack-a-do?" she asked as she laughed.

"I'm just fine Pat," Phil replied.

"We heard what happened yesterday. Are you two okay?" Lynda asked.

"We're doing okay. One of the creatures bit Calista, but she's just fine now," Phil replied.

Pat and Lynda looked at Calista's leg. "Where are the scars from the wound?" Lynda asked.

"Ruth healed me with an herbal mixture and a healing spell," Calista replied softly. "So why are you here?"

"Muggsy called us for another Quest Inc. meeting," Pat answered.

Muggsy came into the dorm and called them for the meeting. When they got to Muggsy's office, all the members of Q.I. were there. They got on the lift in two groups and went down to the Quest Inc. headquarters. As the group had no new conflicts, the meeting was quickly adjourned, so they left headquarters and went back upstairs.

The doorbell rang, and Muggsy answered the door; it was Mr. and Mrs. Matthews.

"We're here to pick up Matt and Zack," Mr. Matthews said as they walked into the house.

Mrs. Matthews handed Muggsy a large envelope and whispered into Muggsy's ear. When Mr. and Mrs. Matthews saw Phil and Calista, they went over to hug them.

"How are you two?" Mrs. Matthews asked.

"Everything's fine," Calista replied.

Matt, Stanchie, Melissa, and Zack came out of the crowd, and Melissa asked Mr. and Mrs. Matthews how they were.

"We're well, dears," Mrs. Matthews answered. "And you?"

"We're fine," the girls replied together.

"You're still coming over for dinner, right, girls?" Mrs. Matthews asked.

"Yes, we are," Stanchie answered.

Matt and Zack gave Phil a pound and turned to Melissa, Calista, Stanchie, and Lisa, hugging them.

"See ya," Zack and Matt called out as they left the house.

The kids went and hung out in the game room and the dorms while Muggsy, Pat, Ruth, and Lynda stayed behind in Muggsy's office. An hour later, Lynda and Pat came out of the office, said good-bye to the kids, and left the orphanage. The day lingered on and slowly turned into night. The kids made their way down to the dining room for dinner. When everyone was done eating, they washed up and went to sleep. Phil spent all night tossing and turning from reliving the experiences of the previous night in his dreams.

The following morning, Phil woke up still sleepy, and he yawned. He went to the bathroom, washed up, and went to the girls' dorm. Lisa and Calista were the only two girls in the room. As she looked at his face, Calista asked him what happened. Phil didn't want her to know about the dreams, so he said it was nothing. The three of them went down for breakfast. As Phil ate, he thought to himself that the noise of all the kids laughing and talking was too loud. He closed his eyes and tried to block out the noise, but it got louder and louder.

When Phil was done eating he quickly went to the kitchen, put his dishes into the sink, and ran out of the dining room. He went outside to the backyard and sat on a lawn chair. It was nice and warm, and a gentle breeze blew against Phil, making the hairs on the back of his neck stand straight up. He sat and thought about the other night, the night he and Calista saw Azazelbog. Why did Azazelbog possess Alex's decaying body? And if his soul wasn't at rest, was that the only reason Azazelbog took his body? Or was Alex special to him? And why did Supay take over his boss, Jeremy?

Calista and Lisa came out to the backyard and joined Phil. As they were sitting there, Phil felt that someone was watching them. He looked around, but nobody was there; however, the feeling wouldn't dissipate. Suddenly, he heard voices all around him. Phil asked the girls if they heard anything, and they said no. The voices got louder and louder, and Azazelbog's voice resonated louder over all the others and echoed through the air.

"You fleshlings will be destroyed, and there's nothing you can do. Your kind will die."

Calista and Lisa asked Phil what was the matter, and Phil said it was nothing, not wanting to worry them. A while later, he went to Muggsy's office and knocked on the door. Muggsy told him to come in.

"What are you going to do?" Phil asked as he took a seat.

"What do you mean by that?" Muggsy asked.

"What are you going to do about what happened to Calista, Ruth, and me?"

"I made a couple of calls to some people, but I'm honestly not sure what to do."

"Okay, Muggsy, I'll talk to you later."

Phil quickly left the room and slowly trotted up the stairs to the boys' dorm. A few minutes later, Lisa and Calista came into the room, and the three of them started talking. As they were sitting there, a piercing cold stabbing feeling swept over Phil's entire body. Phil's eyes slowly rolled back, and something appeared in front of him. It was a woman floating in the air. She had long white flowing hair and pale white skin; she was wearing a long flowing white gown. She stared an endless stare into Phil's eyes.

"I am the oracle Dorbol," she began. "I have come to show you the future of humankind. All these things will come to pass if you and Quest Inc. do not intervene."

"Phil, are you okay?" Calista asked, shaking him softly. "Are you okay?"

Lisa and Calista got up from where they were sitting and ran out of the room.

The oracle folded her hands together and slowly opened them up again; smoke and a bright light came out of her hands and filled the room. The skies were as dark as satin cloth, and there were dragons flying in the sky. Azazelbog and Supay were riding on large dragon-like creatures. The living dead were writhing around, dragging their bodies, feasting on the bodies of the living. The other living people were chained and shackled up together. Supay and Azazelbog got off the dragon creatures and began whipping the living people with long sharp, spiky whips. The world was under the evil power of Azazelbog and Supay. All around them, buildings and houses were smoking and on fire, some totally destroyed.

"There is only one weapon that will help in the fight against Azazelbog and Supay; it's called the Spear of Destiny," Dorbol softly said.

Another bright light shined out of her hand, and an image of a spear appeared; the spear looked old and rusted. It was all metal, with a long narrowed head, and the shaft was more rusted over than the rest of it. At the very bottom of the spear was an old wooden handle.

"There will be a friendly visitor from a great distance away. He will help you find the Spear of Destiny and fight with you against Azazelbog and his great evil," Dorbol said.

The Spear of Destiny faded, and a pyramid appeared. Slowly a spaceship landed on top of the pyramid.

Dorbol softly moaned. "Quest Inc. must get allies and fight or all will be lost."

Suddenly, the oracle vanished. The bright lights and smoke cleared from the room, and Phil fell onto his bed, now all alone.

A couple of minutes later, Lisa and Ruth came into the dorm. Ruth helped Phil up, and the three of them left the room. They went downstairs to Muggsy's office and sat at the desk. Muggsy and Calista came into the office and sat down. Muggsy stared into Phil's eyes and shook her head.

"What just happened?" Muggsy asked.

"I don't know," Phil said quickly. "The girls saw what happened. Why don't you ask them?"

"All we saw were you shaking as if you were having a seizure, and then you stood totally still, as if you were in a trance," Calista said as she looked at Phil.

"Are you serious? You didn't see the pale floating lady in the dorm?" Phil asked angrily. "I'm not crazy."

"I'm sorry. We just didn't see anything," Lisa said.

"Muggsy, I'm not crazy. I know what I saw," Phil said worriedly.

"Okay, just tell me what you saw," Muggsy told him.

Phil started to explain to them what had happened in the dorm, describing what he saw.

"And the spirit specifically said she was an oracle?" Muggsy asked.

"Yes, I'm positive," Phil replied.

"Oracles can only be seen by the person or people they want to talk to and show visions to," Muggsy began to explain. "I did some research after the pope's advisers called and told me that he had a vision too."

"How do you know it's the same vision?" Phil asked.

"The advisers described the same exact vision, and it says that if two people have the same vision, it will come true," Muggsy said.

"I did some research too, and my books say the same thing," Ruth added.

"So this means Quest Inc. has to fight in this war, doesn't it?" Calista asked.

"Yes it does," Muggsy replied as she looked at Phil and Calista. "Would you two join Quest Inc. again?"

"Do we have a choice?" Phil said.

"Lisa, go call the other Q.I. members and tell them I'm having another meeting," Muggsy said.

Lisa got up and left the room, leaving them behind to talk. Five minutes later, voices were echoing through the hall, and Lisa and the other members soon entered the room. Muggsy, Phil, Calista, and Ruth got up, and Muggsy punched in the code. The rickety old lift slowly rose. They all got in and Phil closed the gate. After the lift descended and came to a halt, Phil unlatched the gate and they all got out.

As they sat down, they heard the lift rising again with a loud clanging thud. Lynda and Pat walked into the headquarters and sat down moments later.

"We're sorry we're late," Lynda said.

"That's okay; we were going to wait for you anyway." Muggsy stood up and cleared her throat. "We are all here today because the pope's advisers asked us to go on a mission."

"What's the mission for?" one of the members asked.

"The first part of the mission is to retrieve the Spear of Destiny," Muggsy responded.

"What is the Spear of Destiny, exactly?" Stanchie asked.

"When Jesus Christ died on the cross, one of the guards took his spear and pierced Jesus in the side. His blood spilled onto the spear. Legends and the church say that the same spear has the power to make demons mortal and even kill them," Muggsy explained.

"Why do we have to retrieve the spear?" Melissa asked.

"I was about to explain that. The second part of the mission is to help fight in the war against Satan's son, Azazelbog, and his minion Supay," Muggsy said.

"Hold on. Nobody, including the heads of the church, ever said that Satan had a son," one of the members said.

"Well, the Book of Shadows, also known as the Unholy Bible of the Dead, has references that state Satan does have a son," Ruth said.

"The pope and Phil both had the same vision about Azazelbog taking over the world, enslaving all of mankind, and making our world his new hellish home. Research says that if an oracle gives two people the same vision, the vision will come true."

Some of the members began whispering to each other and looking at Phil.

"If there are no other questions or comments, then this meeting is over," Muggsy said.

After they'd left the Quest Inc. headquarters, Ryan joined some other kids who went to hang out outside. Meanwhile, Muggsy, Lynda, Ruth, and Pat stayed behind in Muggsy's office. Phil, Lisa, and Calista went up to the game room and began playing video games and talking. A little while later, Phil heard the front doorbell ring. A few minutes later, Ruth came into the game room and called to Lisa, Phil, and Calista. They got up and left the room. As they made their way to Muggsy's office, the voices got louder and louder.

Ruth's four friends who had been in the cemetery were standing in the corner of the room. One of the women was the same height as Ruth. She had short blonde hair, and she was wearing black jeans and a black T-shirt. The second woman had long silky straight hair, and she was tall. She wore a black halter top and black sweatpants. The third woman had long curly hair and was slightly chubby, wearing a long dark dress. The fourth woman was clearly the youngest, and she had beautiful locks of silky flowing blonde hair. She was wearing a leather halter top and a leather skirt. Muggsy told them all to sit down, and they did as directed.

"This is Becky, Denise, Gina, and Zoe; I am part of their coven," Ruth said. "They would like to join Quest Inc. and fight against Azazelbog and Supay."

"How can I trust them?" Muggsy asked. "Just because they helped you guys in the cemetery ..."

"In our defense, Azazelbog and Supay tried to hurt our families!" Zoe exclaimed in an upsetting voice "Their followers attacked us and our families after we helped Ruth, Phil, and Calista, at the cemetery that night."

"I'm not really sure I can let you join Quest Inc., but you can certainly fight with us against Azazelbog and Supay," Muggsy said. She stood up and shook the women's hands before they all left the room.

CHAPTER 5

Extraterrestrial Visitors

A couple of days had passed, and it was now July. Phil turned on the TV and sat on the couch; a news reporter was reporting from Egypt. As thunder and lightning rumbled through the sky, she said that there were lightning storms all around Egypt. Phil turned off the TV and went to Muggsy's office. He punched in the code, and the rickety lift came up. Moments later, he was slowly walking through the narrow hallway and entering the Quest Inc. headquarters. Ryan was working with test tubes and computer equipment, and Muggsy was talking with him. Ryan asked Phil for his help.

"What are you working on?" Phil asked as he approached.

"I'm making a demon signature locator," Ryan replied. "Will you hand me that little circuit board?"

Phil handed it to Ryan. He put it onto the other one, and Phil welded both circuit boards together. Azazelbog and one of the gothic teens abruptly appeared right in front of them.

"I come to get what belongs to me," Azazelbog said as he turned and looked at the refrigerator. "I am calling you. Come to me now."

The freezer started shaking violently and then exploded. Muggsy gaped at Azazelbog in astonishment, clearly startled that Azazelbog had taken over Alex's body and was standing in front of her. Tears started rolling down her cheeks as she stared into Azazelbog's eyes, and angry emotions clearly overcame her. She grabbed a knife from one of the tables and ran toward Azazelbog. Azazelbog waved his left hand through the air, and a gust of wind blew, hitting Ryan, Muggsy, and Phil, causing them to fly into a wall.

"Come to me now!" Azazelbog exclaimed again.

At that second, a red light quickly began flashing on the cryogenic containment unit and smoke bellowed out of it. The red light flashed faster and faster, and the unit exploded. The ice around the slimy ooze quickly melted, and the ooze crawled across the floor. It crawled up the gothic girl and slid back down her entire body, covering her. The ooze started going into the girl's throat, and a few minutes later, the girl's eyes rolled back and she smiled and laughed evilly. She looked at Muggsy, Phil, and Ryan before turning to Azazelbog.

"I am ready to serve you, my lord," the girl said in a deep demonic voice.

Azazelbog turned and smirked at Muggsy and Phil. "We will see each other soon," Azazelbog snarled.

Flames surrounded Azazelbog and the girl, engulfing them. When the fire died, they both had disappeared. Muggsy frowned and slammed her fists onto the conference table.

"Tomorrow is the second of July. I'm going to make arrangements to go to Egypt," Muggsy said in an upset voice.

Ryan continued to work on the demon signature locator as Phil and Muggsy left the headquarters. When they both got back to the office, Phil was about to leave when Muggsy stopped him.

"I have something for you," she said to him.

She unlocked a large metal cabinet and handed him the sword and crossbow that Buzz had given him.

"I thought you would've gotten rid of these."

"I just couldn't get rid of something Buzz gave you. And besides, I figured you would need to use these again."

"Do you still have the mannequin?"

"Of course I do."

Muggsy opened a large cabinet again and took out a mannequin. It was all cut up and it had holes in it. She handed it to him.

"Thank you."

"You're welcome."

Phil took the crossbow, sword, and mannequin up to the boys' dorm and started to polish the sword. When he was finished polishing it, he put it back into its scabbard and tied it to his back. Then he took the crossbow and mannequin and went out to the backyard. He tied the mannequin up to a tree, took the sword out of the scabbard, and began practicing. With each slash of the sword in the mannequin, Phil's anger and sadness rose like a lethal serpent. A half hour later, he put the sword back into the scabbard. He took some arrows and loaded the crossbow, and then he aimed the crossbow at the mannequin and shot it up with arrows.

A little while later, Lisa came out to the backyard and told Phil that Muggsy was calling another Q.I. meeting. They both went inside, and Phil went up to the boys' dorm and put the sword and crossbow under his bed. He then met Lisa in Muggsy's office to head down to the headquarters. When they got there, they both sat down and the meeting began. Muggsy explained to the others what had happened to Ryan, Phil, and her earlier in the day. She also spoke about the mission to Egypt. A half an hour later, the meeting ended. After they left the headquarters, Phil found a ball, and he, Lisa, Ryan, and Calista went to the backyard and played basketball.

Early that afternoon, they went back inside to play video games. The telephone rang, and moments later, one of the boys came into the game room and told Phil the phone call was for him. Phil went to the boys' dorm and picked up the phone. After he ended the call, he went back to the game room.

"Do you want to come to the park with me?" Phil asked.

"Okay, we'll come," Calista replied.

"Do you want to come too?" Phil asked Ryan.

"I really can't. I have to finish working on the locator," Ryan replied.

Ryan left the room, and Phil went to the boys' dorm to get his skateboard. He then went to Muggsy's office and said, "Do you mind if Lisa, Calista, and I go to the park?" Phil asked.

"Okay, you can go, but be the three of you need to be back by six thirty," Muggsy replied. "And make sure that Stanchie and Melissa come home with you as well."

"Okay, thanks Muggsy."

He went to the den and waited for the girls. When they got to the park, Zack and Matt gave Phil pounds, and the three of them began to shred. Lisa, Stanchie, Calista, and Melissa sat down and started to talk.

"We were surprised that Muggsy let you come after what happened to you this morning," Matt said.

"I thought the same thing," Phil said. "The only problem is that we have to get back by six thirty."

"That only gives us about two hours, so let's shred it up," Zack said.

A little while later, an ice cream truck came by and stopped in front of the main entrance. The boys skated over to the truck and got sodas for themselves and bottles of water for the girls. They gave the girls the water and continued to shred, and at six o'clock, they left the park. A couple of minutes later, they reached Zack and Matt's home. They both kissed Melissa and Stanchie and gave Phil a pound; both boys hugged Lisa and Calista and went inside.

When the others got back to the orphanage, they went to their dorms, changed their clothes, and went down for dinner. Right after Phil was done eating, he gathered up the dishes and took them to the kitchen. Doris was there washing dishes.

"How are you doing? I haven't talked to you in a while," Phil said.

"I'm doing okay. Same old thing, different day," Doris replied as she smiled. "I heard what happened this morning."

"Yeah, that was really crazy," Phil said, "Did you notice that Muggsy is acting strange?"

"She's been getting progressively worried for the past year about everything. And ever since this morning, she's been even more worried."

"Well, I guess I understand. I'll talk to you later."

"It was nice talking to you again. I'll see you later."

Phil went up to the dorm to lie down on his bed. Seconds later, Muggsy came into the dorm and turned off the light. Phil closed his eyes and slowly fell asleep. At four o'clock in the morning, Muggsy came into the dorm, opened up the blinds, and woke Phil up. He yawned and quickly looked at the clock.

"Why did you call me so early?" Phil asked sleepily.

"You have to get ready right now. We're leaving in about an hour," Muggsy whispered.

"Get ready for what? Where are we going?"

"We're going to Egypt. Now wash up and meet me in headquarters."

Muggsy left the dorm, and Phil lazily got out of his bed and made his way to the bathroom. Minutes later, he was down in Muggsy's office. Phil punched in the code, and the lift slowly came up. When he got to the headquarters, Muggsy and Ryan were there waiting for him. Muggsy walked Phil to a closet. They doors opened automatically and they went inside.

"I just dusted off your Q.I. suit. Suit up and meet me by the conference desk," Muggsy said. "I arranged the plane yesterday. Ryan prepared some new weapons for the mission; I'll let Ryan tell you more about them."

"I have made an assortment of ass kickery for your enjoyment. First, the Mini Stake cannon. This baby could pump out six silver stakes at a time from a mile away," Ryan began explaining. "This is my favorite. I call it the hush hound. It's a crossbow that reloads automatically and shoots multiple arrows at a time. And finally, you know about the Demon Signature Locator."

"Who's going on this mission?" Phil asked.

"Just Ruth, you, Ryan, and I are going," Muggsy replied.

A few minutes later, Ruth joined them, and Ryan showed them how to use the new weapons and equipment. A half hour later, after grabbing a quick bite to eat, the four of them left headquarters and quickly left the house. They jumped into the Hummer, and Muggsy pulled out of the driveway. Because it was only five o'clock in the morning, the streets were dark and quiet. A half hour later, they were at JFK airport, and they took a small narrow side road to the cargo hold area. Muggsy parked the Hummer right outside the airplane hangar, and Muggsy's pilot friend walked up to them and shook their hands.

The pilot led them into the hangar and over to a small plane. He opened the plane's hatch door, and they quickly went inside. The interior of the plane was cramped; there was only room for five people to sit. A booming voice came over the speakers.

"Everybody sit down and strap up. We're going to take off in a minute," the captain said.

The plane hangar workers quickly opened the hangar doors, and the plane's engine roared to life. The plane slowly pulled out of the hangar. A couple of minutes later, the plane reached the runway. The plane went faster and faster down the runway before quickly soaring into the air.

"If you want, you can take off your seat belts now," the pilot said over the speaker.

"Who's watching the others?" Phil asked Muggsy.

"Toby and Doris said they'll take care of the kids until we get back," Muggsy replied.

Ruth began chanting an incantation, and Ryan asked her what she was doing.

"What are you doing?" Ryan asked.

"I am just casting some protective spells," Ruth replied.

"Why are you doing that?" Muggsy asked.

"It is to protect us from Azazelbog trying to harm us," Ruth replied.

The sun slowly began to rise, and its light quickly filled the plane. They made a quick pit stop in London to refuel and then continued on their journey. Ruth, Phil, Muggsy, and Ryan were talking and laughing with each other. As the day went on, the sky turned cloudy and dark, and it became a full-on thunderstorm.

Eight hours had passed very slowly, and the day turned into night. The moon shined brightly, and the stars twinkled in the sky.

A little while later, the four of them closed their eyes and went to sleep. The captain put the plane on autopilot and went to the restroom. Everything was calm until the plane started to shake. The passengers opened their eyes and looked at each other. The pilot stuck his head out of the cockpit door.

"Don't worry. It's just some turbulence," the pilot said.

About two hours later, they reached Cairo International Airport and slowly began to descend. When the plane came to a halt, everybody got out. Suddenly, a Jeep Wrangler pulled up in front of them. Jean-Luke, the international Q.I. operative, walked over to them and shook their hands.

"Do you still have the radio I gave you?" Muggsy asked Phil.

"Yes, I do," Phil replied as he took a radio out of his utility belt.

"Are you four ready to go?" Jean-Luke asked.

"Yes, we are," Muggsy replied.

"Where are you going, my friends?" Jean-Luke asked as they drove away.

"We're going to the pyramid tomb of King Tut," Phil quickly replied.

"Are you sure it's that pyramid?" Muggsy asked.

"Yes, I'm positive," Phil replied.

The Wrangler quickly zipped its way through the streets of Cairo, making its way to the desert.

When they got to the desert, it was as if the Jeep were a jet ski and they were surfing on a vast, endless sea of sand. The sand was getting thrown around as the Wrangler drove faster and faster. Just then, the Demon Signature Locator started to blink and beep loudly. Ryan stared at the locator and frowned.

"The D.S.L. indicates that there's a demon nearby and by the looks of the gauge and the sound of the D.S.L. it's pretty powerful," Ryan said.

Ryan and Phil looked outside and saw two huge bumps in the sand moving toward the Jeep, and they slammed into it. Two large demons probably sent by Azazelelbog jumped out of the sand. The demons appeared to be made out of sand; they had razor-sharp claws and jagged spikes protruding from their skin. The demons' white hellish eyes darted at Phil as they grinned at the Jeep. The demons jumped back into the sand and swam toward the Wrangler; they both rammed the Jeep again and swam away. Phil got up from his seat.

"What are you doing!" Muggsy yelled. "What are you thinking?"

"You know me—I don't think," Phil replied.

A second later, he jumped out of the moving Jeep and rolled onto the sand. Phil quickly got up, loaded silver stakes into the mini stake cannon, and pulled his sword out of the scabbard. The two demons jumped out of the sand, knocking Phil onto his back. Both demons were about to bite his legs when some unseen force stopped them. Phil looked around and saw that the Wrangler had stopped a few yards away. Ruth was running toward him chanting a spell. She took her staff and hit the demons hard; the demons fell back and started growling.

"I dipped your sword and the silver stakes in holy water. Holy water does not kill demons, but it does hurt them," Ruth called out.

Phil shot one of the demons in the stomach, and it fell on its back, grabbing its stomach and crying in agony as the wound began to sizzle. Ruth waved her staff in the air and struck it down hard into the sand; a gust of wind blew, hitting the demons. The demons were thrown into the air, and they hit the sand hard. One of the demons dove into the sand and swam toward them. When it jumped out of the sand, Phil plunged his sword into the demon and then shot it with the mini stake cannon.

The demon screamed and cried in agony, and then both demons dove into the sand again and swarm away. Muggsy ran over to Phil and slapped him on the back of his head.

"What the hell were you thinking? We have to get to the pyramid alive!" Muggsy exclaimed.

"I was thinking about stopping those demons from killing us," Phil said.

"Well, you both did well," Muggsy said.

Muggsy smiled at Phil and Ruth, also patting them on their shoulders. They got into the Jeep and drove away. As the Jeep Wrangler moved faster and faster, the breezy air whipped through their hair, blowing it everywhere. As they got closer to the pyramid of King Tut, claps of thunder rumbled through the afternoon sky. When they reached the pyramid and climbed out of the Jeep, they saw a person in the distance, also making his way toward the pyramid.

As the person got closer, it was evident that he was a tall older man with dark eyes and wild, wavy brown hair. He looked poor, for he was dirty and his thin clothes were ripped. The man walked right over to them and collapsed. A moment later, he slowly got up and asked them for some water; Phil handed the man a water canteen, and the man began drinking. The afternoon sky suddenly turned dark, and lightning lit up the sky as clapping thunder rumbled.

The sand under them started to shake, and the pyramid shook as well. An enormous storm cloud appeared over the pyramid, covering the whole thing. The pyramid shook even harder, and steel beams shot out of all four sides of it and bent upward; electricity started shooting through the steel beams. Moments later, a spaceship began to descend from the cloud, and it landed on top of the steel beams. The spaceship looked like an upside down pyramid that was made of metal and steel. All around the ship were strange hieroglyphics. Four circular orbs were circling the ship.

The poor man quickly dropped to his knees, put his hands together, and began praying. The bottom of the spaceship began to open, and a bright light shot out of it. A shiny round metal orb came out of the opening and flew over the poor man's head. The orb opened, and dark purple slimy ooze slid out of it. It fell on top of the poor man, covering his entire body. When the ooze slid into the man's mouth, his eyes rolled back. The others grabbed their weapons and aimed them at the man.

"Do not fear. I come in peace," the thing said, using the man's voice.

"Shut the hell up. How can we really know that you come here in peace? One of you things has joined Azazelbog, Satan's son!" Muggsy said.

"Please let me explain," the alien said. "My name is Luca. I am part of a shapeless race of beings from the planet Zebigale."

"Why haven't any of us heard of the planet Zebigale?" Phil asked.

"My world is in a galaxy that is seven thousand light years away from your universe," Luca replied.

"What was that one that went and joined Azazelbog?" Muggsy asked.

"That must have been my brother Degalfade; he alone has betrayed my brethren and sisters. Our race is a peaceful one, but Degalfade turned on all of us, and now only a few of my kind remain alive."

"In a vision I had, it showed that an extraterrestrial being is supposed to help us. Are you the being? If so, how are you going to help us?" Phil questioned as he lowered his crossbow.

"Yes, I am; I have the map that leads to the Spear of Destiny," Luca answered, "I would like to fight by your side in the war also."

"We'll see about that," Muggsy said.

"How did you get the map, anyway?" Ryan asked.

"Well, many decades ago, one of the brethren of my planet came to this planet to study humans, and in doing so, he received the map to keep it safe," Luca replied. Luca whistled in a high pitch, and another orb came out of the opening of the spaceship and floated over to him. He waved his hands over the orb, and it fell to the ground with a loud thud. He waved over the orb again, and the spaceship cloaked itself as it disappeared. Luca quickly picked up the orb off the ground, and they all got into the Jeep and drove away. An hour later, they were at the airport and boarding the plane. The plane pulled out of the hangar; it went faster and faster down the runway, slowly soaring into the air.

They all started talking, and Luca told them about his home planet. The sky started growing dark, and they closed their eyes and tried to get some sleep. Twelve hours later, they got back to New York and went straight to the orphanage. When they got there, Pat and Lynda were there waiting in Muggsy's office.

"Why are you here so early?" Phil asked.

"Muggsy called us from the Hummer and told us to come over," Pat replied.

"Hello, you must be Lynda and Pat. Young Phil has told me so much about you two," Luca said as he shook their hands. "I am Luca."

Toby arrived, and they all got into the lift and went to the Quest Inc. headquarters. Luca remained standing while the others sat down. Luca took the orb, put it on the table, and placed one finger on it; he pressed down on the orb, and it slightly lit up. The top of the orb split into four pieces, and a second later, it opened up wide, revealing a wooden object. The object was slightly long and resembled a rolling pin. It had strange writings and hieroglyphics on it.

"Is that the map? I've never seen writing or hieroglyphics like those in any culture in the world," Toby said, admiring them.

"My brethren that originally visited your planet received the map that led to the Spear of Destiny. To keep the map from being taken by evil, he destroyed the original and made this. This is the ancient tongue of my world," Luca explained.

"How long will it take to fabricate a map that we can understand?" Muggsy asked.

"I can try to have it done in two days with Toby and Luca's help," Ryan replied.

They left headquarters, leaving Ryan alone. After they left Muggsy's office, Muggsy showed Luca the guest room he was to stay in. The sun was just coming up, and Doris was coming down from her room. As introductions were made, Doris smiled and shook hands with Luca.

"I just woke up and checked on the kids," Doris said. "I'll see you later. I'm going to go make breakfast." Doris smiled at them again and slowly made her way to the kitchen.

Phil went upstairs to the boys' dorm and changed out of his Q.I. suit. He went back down to headquarters and put the suit away. He saw that Ryan and Luca were working, so he left as quickly and quietly as he could. He went to the den and lay on one of the sofas, staring out the window. Calista walked into the room and kissed him on the forehead. She sat down next to him.

Phil told her all about the mission and Luca. Isaiah soon came to tell them that Doris was calling them for breakfast. Calista and Phil got up, and the three of them left the room. When they were done eating, Phil and Calista went up to the game room and played video games. A while later, Isaiah, Madison, and Brandon joined them.

"Do you realize that the slimy ooze we found at O.L.S was actually an alien?" Phil said, going on to describe what they'd experienced. "Luca and the alien were of the same extraterrestrial species."

"What is Luca like?" Isaiah asked.

"Emotional. He's like any other person," Phil replied.

As the day drew on, there was talk amongst the kids about Luca and the reason he was there. Most of the kids thought Luca was honest about helping, but a few of them thought that he was evil. Later that afternoon, Muggsy called a Q.I. conference, and Luca introduced himself to everyone, easing the people's thoughts. When the conference was over, Phil went to the backyard and shot hoops by himself. A little while later, Luca came outside and walked over to him.

"May I see the ball?" Luca asked, "I would like to show you something."

Phil handed him the ball, and as Luca stared at the ball, it slowly floated into the air and spun around.

"How are you doing that?" Phil asked.

"My whole species can control any material object, but it takes a lot of work to do it," Luca said quietly. "We will all have to work hard to succeed."

"What are you trying to say?" Phil asked.

"Muggsy told me how proud she was of you when you reformed Quest Inc., but you abruptly and left Quest Inc. just because your best friend Alex had died. You can't just stop working on something because things go wrong. That's when you take everything you have and work even harder at it."

Tears rolled down Phil's cheeks, and Luca held him and consoled him until it began to grow dark. Then the two went inside.

CHAPTER 6

The Real Voyage of Christopher Columbus

The following day, Phil woke up and slowly looked around. All the other boys had left the room already. He yawned loudly and jumped out of bed. After he'd had breakfast, he carried his dishes into the kitchen and saw Doris at the sink, scrubbing caked-on food from one of the dishes. She saw Phil and smiled. They chatted for a few minutes.

Phil found Lisa, Isaiah, and Calista in the den, and the four of them went up to the game room to hang out. As they talked, Phil racked up the pool balls. After they'd played a game, which Lisa won, a group of the younger kids came into the game room. The four of them left.

"Where did Luca go?" Calista asked.

"He went with Ruth to see Lynda and Pat," Phil answered.

"Where are Stanchie and Melissa, anyway?" Calista asked.

"They went to the park to meet Matt and Zack."

"The four of them have been hanging out a lot lately," Calista said. "Do you think it's going to get serious between them?"

"I think they're already serious," Lisa replied.

"That's so cute," Calista said.

"I'll be back," Phil interjected. "I have to talk to Muggsy."

Phil went down to Muggsy's office and knocked on the door. Muggsy said to come in.

"Do you think that Lisa, Brandon, Madison, Isaiah, Calista, and I could go to the park?" Phil asked.

"Okay, but be back in three hours," Muggsy replied.

"Are Ryan and Luca done making the map?" Phil asked.

"No, but I think they're almost done."

"Okay I'll see you later."

As Phil got up and started to leave, Muggsy stopped him. "Just make sure that Stanchie and Melissa come back home with you."

"Okay, I will." He left the office and met the others in the den.

On their way to the park, they stopped at Dunkin' Donuts and got some iced coffees cream and shakes. When they got to the park, they found Zack and Matt, and the boys started skating. Two hours later, they walked to Zack and Matt's home; the two boys kissed Stanchie and Melissa before heading into their house. When the others got back to the orphanage, they washed up and hung out in the den. A little while later, Muggsy came to the den and joined the kids. There was a sudden knock on the door. It was Luca.

"Hey Luca, why don't you join us?" Muggsy asked as she moved to an empty sofa.

"You said your people know the whole history of planet earth," Isaiah said to him. "Are you just fascinated about the voyage of Christopher Columbus?"

"Yes, I am, but only my brethren know the real story behind the voyage of Columbus," Luca replied.

"What do you mean by the real voyage of Columbus?" Ryan asked.

"Well, his whole voyage started out with one vision. Would you like to hear about the real journey?" Luca replied.

"We would really like that, but hold on," Muggsy said. She left the room and returned minutes later with Doris and the other kids. They all sat down staring at Luca, excitedly waiting for the story. He smiled at them and told them the tale.

"*It was three long sleepless nights of tossing and turning for Christopher Columbus, and the third night was the worst. He woke up in a cold sweat from a vivid vision. In the vision, he had charted a voyage to a distant land to speak to the head of a native tribe and the natives would bestow a gift unto him. So the following day, he consulted with his closest friend, and he decided to charter the expedition to the new land.*"

All of the children, Muggsy, and Doris were sitting still, wide-eyed, mouths gaping wide, taking in all the words of Luca's story. Soft beads of rain droplets were gently falling outside. Just then, the telephone rang, but Muggsy told them to ignore the phone, so Luca continued his story.

"*When Christopher Columbus reached the distant land, it was just as the vision had told. The chief of the native tribe took Columbus aside and gave him a gift of a special case. The case was made of animal hide that was stitched together. Columbus opened the case to reveal a map. The chief of the native tribe explained to Columbus that the map led to the location of the Spear of Destiny. The chief also explained that he had a vision of Columbus crossing the ocean to Egypt. In Egypt, Columbus would have a meeting with an extraterrestrial and give him the map to keep it safe.*

"*Not heeding the chief's warning, he returned home to Europe. Two days after his return home, Christopher Columbus had a vision similar to the chief of the natives. So that very night, he went to his closest friend, and they had a meeting. The following day, he chartered a ship for a secret journey to Egypt. The crew was very small, only consisting of eight people. After a tiring and long week's journey, they finally got to Egypt. After arriving at King Tut's pyramid, he met with one of the brethren of my planet and gave him the map to the Spear of Destiny. He told my brethren to keep the map safe, and Columbus returned home to continue with his many adventures.*"

For the rest of the day, all the kids were talking about Luca's story.

CHAPTER 7

Return to the Past

The following day, Phil went to the park and met Matt and Zack. They went over to the handball courts and played handball. After they also played basketball for a while, they sat around and talked. As more and more people came to the park, Phil, Matt, and Zack got on their skateboards. At five o'clock, the boys stopped shredding and left the park.

When they got to the orphanage, Phil unlocked the front door and they went inside. They went up to the game room and played PlayStation 3 and pool. It wasn't long before Muggsy came in to tell them that dinner was ready. Muggsy turned to Zack and Matt. "Your mother called, and she said you can stay for dinner."

They went down to the dining room and grabbed plates. Phil got a veggie burger and grilled mushrooms and sat down to eat. Melissa and Stanchie came and sat down next to them, kissing Zack and Matt. When he was done eating, Phil went to the boys' dorm, changed into his pajamas, and lay down on his bed. Zack and Matt came into the dorm and stood next to Phil.

"We have to go. We'll see you later," Matt said.

They both gave Phil a pound and left the room. Phil crawled under the sheets and went to sleep.

When the sun came up, Muggsy ran into the boys' dorm, going over to Phil's bed and shaking him gently.

"Wake up. They finished making the map," Muggsy said.

Phil quickly got out of his bed, washed up, and followed Muggsy to her office. They got onto the rickety old lift and it slowly descended. When they got to the Quest Inc. headquarters, Ryan and Luca were sitting at the conference table. They both saw Muggsy and quickly got up.

"Well, what information do you have for me?" Muggsy asked.

"The map shows that the Spear of Destiny is hidden in Upstate New York, in the town of Schenectady. It was hidden just before the time where Isaiah, Madison, and Brandon came from," Ryan explained "The problem is that over time, the dirt and mud have compacted over the hiding place, and there could also be pavement and even sewage on top of it. If that's the case, we would need contracts and permits just to dig, and that would take weeks, even months."

"Then we'll just have to go to the past to retrieve the spear," Muggsy said.

"It would definitely be easier," Ryan said.

"Ruth and I are definitely going on this mission," Muggsy said.

"I know this is a bad time to ask, but can you reinstate me as junior commander?" Phil asked.

"Of course I can," Muggsy replied.

"I think Lisa, Isaiah, Brandon, Madison, and Calista should help on this mission as well," Phil stated.

"I was just thinking that," Muggsy said. "We're leaving in a couple of hours, so go get ready and tell the others about this mission."

"Okay, Muggsy," Phil said.

When Phil got up to Muggsy's office, he left the room and saw that the others were just coming down for breakfast. He met Calista, and they went to the dining room. When they were done eating, they went up to meet Isaiah, Lisa, Brandon, and Madison in the game room. They sat around and talked. Phil told them about the mission to find the Spear of Destiny and explained that they had to go back to the past. Isaiah, Madison, and Brandon were excited that they were going to see their family and friends; they hadn't seen their parents in a year and a half.

"When are we leaving for this mission?" Isaiah asked.

"Muggsy said we're leaving in a couple of hours, but that was a while ago," Phil replied.

"I guess we should go get ready now," Lisa said.

They went to their respective dorms. Phil, Isaiah, and Brandon put their clothes that they got from the past in a backpack and went down to the living room. A couple of minutes later, the girls came down from their dorm, and they all went down to the Quest Inc. headquarters.

"There you guys are. I was just going to radio Madison and Brandon's parents. Isaiah's too," Muggsy said. "Do you think your parents still have the radio you left them?"

"Of course they do. We just spoke to them last week," Madison said.

Muggsy got the high-frequency radio and turned it on. "This is Muggsy. Can anyone hear me? Is anyone there?"

There was a long staticky silence and then a low purring coming from the other end.

"Oh my gosh, I think that is Cheats," Madison quickly said.

They waited a couple of minutes more.

"We have to leave now, so I guess they aren't going to know that we're coming," Muggsy said.

"Are you guys ready? Because I have to warm up the portal," Ryan commented.

"Yes, we are," Muggsy replied.

"I upgraded the hardware and software for the portal's targeting system. I can send you to exactly where you want to go," Ryan said.

"Send us to this position," Isaiah said. He wrote on a piece of paper and handed it to Ryan.

Ryan went over to the portal and pulled two sheets off it; he walked over to the main console and turned the portal on. He pulled out a keyboard and typed in the directions that Isaiah had given him. Suddenly, the bolts fell off and the prongs turned and shifted; the stone and metal center of the portal turned into a jellied center. A huge gust of wind blew through the headquarters. Muggsy, Phil, Lisa, Isaiah, Brandon, Madison, Calista, and Ruth walked through the portal, and it closed behind them.

A few minutes later, the portal opened up again and spat them out all covered in jelly liquid. They walked down the field, and in the distance, they spotted Cheats the cheetah running around and playing. Isaiah took his fingers and whistled, and it echoed through the air. Cheats turned around and sprinted up the field; he jumped onto Isaiah, Madison, and Brandon and began licking them. He then went over to Phil, Lisa, and Calista and licked them on the face. Cheats stared into Muggsy's eyes and started circling around her. Isaiah walked over to Cheats and rubbed his ears; Cheats layed down on the long blades of grass and purred slowly. Muggsy knelt down and stroked Cheats and he licked her face.

They all headed down to the farm. Brandon and Madison went to the back of the cabin and found a pail of small fish to feed so they began feeding Cheats. Isaiah went into the cabin, found the radios, and gave them to Muggsy. She radioed Ryan and Doris to let them know that they had reached the past safely.

The afternoon sky slowly began to darken, and Cheats lay down in the grass. The stars twinkled, and the moon shone brightly as the night sky turned a dark satin purple. Madison, Isaiah, and Brandon started cleaning up the barn and putting the farm animals away, and Phil went to help them. They all turned at the sound of a wagon in the distance. It was heading toward the farm. Isaiah looked closer and saw his mom with Brandon and Madison's mom and dad.

Isaiah's mom saw them and jumped down out of the wagon. She ran down the field, and when she got to the cabin, she hugged and kissed the kids. When Brandon and Madison's parents got to the cabin, they jumped out of the wagon and hugged and kissed the kids as well.

"Oh my, we missed you kids so much. We thought we would never see you again," Isaiah's mom said.

All of the parents smiled at Muggsy and shook her hand.

"You must be Muggsy. It is such a pleasure to finally meet you," Brandon's mom said.

"Thanks, and the pleasure is mine," Muggsy said.

Ruth smiled at Brandon and Madison's parents.

"We missed you, old friend," Brandon's father said.

"I have missed the three of you a lot as well," Ruth replied.

"How are you doing, Mother?" Isaiah asked.

"It is hard since your father passed away but I have good friends to take care of me," she replied as tears rolled down her face.

"We are actually here because we have to retrieve the Spear of Destiny," Brandon said.

"You mean the Dagger of Destiny," Isaiah's mother said.

"What do you mean by the Dagger of Destiny?" Muggsy asked.

"Well, before they hid the spear, the spearhead broke off from the shaft; so they fashioned the spearhead into a dagger," Isaiah's mother replied. She explained the full story and history of the Dagger of Destiny through the years until the final hiding place. They sat listening intently to every word as she unraveled the tale.

"How do you know so much about the Dagger of Destiny?" Muggsy asked.

"I should know the history of it," Isaiah's mother said. "My grandfather led the quest to hide it."

"How long are you staying here?" Brandon and Madison's mother asked.

"Just until we find the Spear of Destiny—the dagger, I mean," Muggsy replied, "We should be leaving in a couple of days."

"We must talk to you, Brandon," his father said, staring into his eyes. "It is concerning Lillian."

"What happened? Is she okay?"

"She is just fine. It is just that …"

"Can we talk later, then? We have to go purchase some clothing for Muggsy."

"You can go to town tomorrow morning." Isaiah's mother said. "We going to have supper now and go to sleep."

Isaiah tied the horses in the stables, and they all went into the cabin; the boys set the table, and everyone sat down to eat.

"What are we having for supper?" Isaiah asked.

"We are having rabbit stew," Brandon's mother said as she took a large pot off the fire pit.

She dished out the stew, and everyone started eating. When they were done eating, Isaiah's mother, Liza, and the kids took the dirty dishes and went to the stream. Liza washed the dishes while the kids dried them. When they got back to the cabin, everybody went to sleep.

In the morning, they all washed up and had breakfast. When they were done eating, Phil and Isaiah took two horses out of the stables and harnessed them to the wagon. When everyone was in the wagon, they headed to town. After Isaiah tied up the horses, they went to Lillian's clothing shop. There was a little boy running around inside.

"Lillian, there someone here to see you!" Brandon's mother called out.

"Okay Liza, I will be there in a second!" she called back. Lillian replied.

A second later, Lillian came out of the back, and she stared at Brandon; she then ran over and hugged and kissed him. Liza picked up the little boy and began playing with him.

"Who is that little boy?" Brandon asked.

"That is your son. His name is Daniel," Lillian replied.

"How is that little boy my son? We have only been gone for one and a half years. He looks older."

"Brandon, you have been gone for five years," His mother said.

Brandon cleared his throat and stared at Muggsy; Muggsy shrugged her shoulders as she looked back at him.

"Ryan must have forgotten to set the time grid," Phil suggested.

"So … he is my son," Brandon said as a tear rolled down his cheeks.

"Come, let us say hello to your father," Liza said as she handed Daniel to Brandon.

Brandon held little Daniel tightly and hugged and kissed him. "Hey, big guy. Do you know what? I am your father."

Daniel smiled at Brandon.

"Muggsy, follow me to the back. I will show you some clothing," Lillian said.

Lillian led Muggsy into the back while the others were playing with Daniel. A little later, Muggsy came out of the back wearing a dress and a cloak around her neck. A girl walked into the shop, smiled at Lillian, and went to the back of the shop. Lillian picked Daniel up, and she led them out of the shop. They walked around for a while, just talking and laughing together. They finally made their way to Ruth's old tavern and sat at a bench.

One of the tavern maidens came over to them. She gave them a bowl of spiced nuts and walked away. Minutes later, the tavern maiden returned with mugs of ale for them. An hour later, they left the tavern and walked around town.

"How long are you staying for?" Lillian asked.

"Only for a couple of days," Brandon replied. "Why do you and Daniel come to the time to come with us?"

"I cannot. My mother has fallen ill, and I have to take care of her," Lillian replied.

"Is Lord Devon still king?" Isaiah asked.

"Yes, he is, and he has recently re-wedded," Liza answered.

Madison and Brandon started to laugh. "We thought he would never get re-wedded," Brandon said.

"Liza, how is the tavern doing?" Ruth asked.

"It is doing really well," Liza replied.

"We better go get ready for the quest for the Dagger of Destiny," Muggsy said.

Lillian and Daniel kissed Brandon and embraced him; they bid farewell to the others and went back to the shop. They got onto the wagon, and Liza took hold of the reins. When they got back to the farm, they got down from the wagon, and Isaiah and Calista tied the horses in the stables. Brandon and Madison went and looked for their mother and father, Anna and Joseph. They were feeding the animals. The others went and played with Cheats. When Brandon and Madison's parents were done caring feeding the animals, they went into the cabin.

There was a knock at the door, and Liza answered it; it was a royal guard. The guard handed Liza a rolled-up parchment and walked away. Liza closed the door, unfolded the parchment, and read it.

To the Warriors of Raw,

I have received word that Isaiah, Madison, Brandon, and their friends have returned. I am holding a banquet, and I would like all of you to come.

Sincerely,
Lord Devon

Liza gave the parchment to the others, and they read it.

"Do we have time to go to the banquet?" Isaiah asked.

"I think we do," Muggsy replied, "and I think it would be nice to go to it."

Isaiah and Brandon fed Cheats and played with him, and a short while later, they all started getting ready for the banquet. When they were ready, Joseph took the horses out of the stables and hitched the wagon to them. When they reached the town, it was eerily quiet and empty. They followed the side road to the castle. At the end of the road was a large gate with guards guarding it. The guards opened the gate, and they rode through. Upon arriving at the main court of the castle, they got off the wagon and tied up the horses.

The court was busy with the noise of people hustling and bustling around. They slowly made their way to the banquet hall, where they found Lord Devon talking to some ladies and gentlemen. Lord Devon saw them and came over to greet and hug them.

"It is nice to see you back from the time to come," Devon said.

"How did you know that we were back?" Isaiah asked.

"One of the guards told me that they saw you this morning," Devon replied. "Wait right here. I want you to meet some people." He left and returned a minute later with a woman and a girl.

"This lovely maiden is the woman I have wedded and the new queen, Lady Gloria; and this is her daughter and my new daughter, Donna," Devon said.

"It is very nice to meet you," Gloria said.

"Nice to meet you," Donna said.

They both shook their hands, and Donna looked at Isaiah with a twinkle in her eyes. Kitchen maidens came into the banquet hall with trays of food. Once they left, everyone sat down and began to eat.

"Would you like to get to know each other?" Donna asked Isaiah.

"I would like that. We can talk after we eat," Isaiah replied.

When all had finished eating, Isaiah and Donna left the banquet hall.

"How does it feel to be royalty?" Isaiah asked.

"I guess it is fun. I mean, my mother and I were not always of high class," Donna said.

"What do you mean by that?"

"Well, we used to be lower class, and we lived in the edge of town near the Moily swamp."

"Oh my gosh, Brandon, Madison, and I used to play in Moily swamp all the time. We must have run into each other at one time."

They spent a long while talking and laughing with each other, and they looked at each other with a twinkle in their eyes. Isaiah slowly held Donna's hands and kissed her on the cheek. After walking for some time, they reached a large door with golden floral trim on it.

"Well, this is my quarters. Would you like to come in and talk more?"

"Okay, that would be nice."

Isaiah and Donna held hands and went into the room, and Donna closed the door behind them.

An hour later, Isaiah came out of the room holding Donna's hand, and they went to the throne room. Everyone was still talking, so Isaiah and Donna sat down and joined in the conversation. Ruth and Muggsy were explaining to Lord Devon why they were in the past. A little later, Lord Devon bid them farewell, and they left the banquet hall. When they got back to the farm, they tied up the horses and went into the cabin to talk about the mission.

"We should start looking for the Dagger of Destiny tomorrow at dawn," Muggsy suggested. She took out the map and showed it to Liza and Ruth.

"I do not know if we would be safe in the Valley of the Lost," Liza said.

"Why is it called the Valley of the Lost, and why is it not safe there?" Phil asked.

"The answer for both inquiries is that no one has returned from that valley, ever," Anna replied.

"There are too many dangerous perils in the Valley of the Lost," Ruth said, "and there is a small chance we may die."

"We traveled to the Valley of the Lost for our first quest and we only made it out alive with the help of our allies," Madison said.

"Well, that is a chance we have to take," Muggsy said. "We should get to bed; we have a big day ahead of us."

"We will go sleep with Cheats outside," Isaiah said.

"That is not necessary," Liza said. But Muggsy, Ruth, the kids, and Cheats ran out into the field and went to sleep.

They all woke up before dawn, and the kids let the animals out; they all washed up and ate breakfast afterward. When they were done eating, they got their weapons ready for the mission. Muggsy, Phil, Lisa, and Calista changed into the Q.I. suits; and Isaiah, Madison, and Brandon changed into the Warriors of Raw armor.

"It feels good to be back in this armor," Brandon said.

From a distance, they heard wagons and marching coming toward the farm. Five minutes later, the sounds stopped in front of the cabin. There was a knock at the door; it was Lord Devon and the royal guards. They were wearing battle armor that was packed with weapons.

"We are here to assist you on this quest," Devon said.

"Thanks for the offer, but we don't need help," Phil said.

"You have helped me once before, and now it is time to repay the debt," Devon replied.

"Yeah, but we are up against Azazelbog, the son of the devil himself, along with his other demons," Phil said.

"We are well aware of that," Devon said.

"Did you talk to Lady Gloria and Donna and say your good-byes to them, just in case something happens?" Muggsy asked.

"Yes, I have," Lord Devon answered, and he turned to Isaiah. "Donna told me to tell you that she gives her heart to you."

Isaiah smiled and started to blush.

Muggsy showed Devon and the guards how to use the mini stake cannons and the hush hounds.

"Can you handle using those weapons?" Muggsy asked.

"We will manage them," Devon answered.

Cheats skulked over to Isaiah and Liza and let out a long purr.

"We are sorry, but we cannot let you come with us," Liza said.

Cheats began to purr sadly, and Isaiah began petting him. Seconds later, they left the cabin, and Joseph walked to the wagon.

"No," Lord Devon called out.

"We are not taking the wagon?" Anna asked.

"No, the wagon will only slow us down," Lord Devon said.

As they mounted the horses and rode away, and Cheats crept back into the cabin.

Chapter 8

The Dagger of Destiny

As the day slowly passed, the heat of the sun and the humidity began taking a toll on their tired bodies. The sounds of the galloping horses filled the air as they entered the forest. What felt like hours were only minutes, and now and then, they stopped to drink out of their water canteens and rest. A couple of hours later, the forest cleared away and they were in swampy land. The sound of frogs croaking and buzzing insects filled the air, and it began driving them crazy. As they got to the middle of the swamp, they jumped down off the horses and walked the rest of the way through it.

Late afternoon eventually gave way to night, and the twinkling stars slowly began coming out. They reached the end of the swamp and rode their horses again. Two hours later, they finally reached the Valley of the Lost. It was a vast desert with raging winds that blew heavily. The rotting skeletons of fallen warriors littered the sandy floor of the wasteland.

"We better set up camp for tonight," Ruth suggested. "I will take first watch."

The others set up two tents and rested while Ruth sat in front of the tents and kept watch. As the night drew on, it took all her might to stay awake. A few hours later, Isaiah came out of the tent and took over watch. In the morning, Isaiah went into the tents and woke them up.

"Thanks for taking that last watch," Ruth said.

"It was no problem," Isaiah answered.

They folded up the tents and tied everything up on the horses, ready to ride into the Valley of the Lost.

"The map shows that we on the right path," Ruth called out.

They crossed a huge sand plateau and sand dunes. They wrapped handkerchiefs around their faces so the sand that was blowing in the air wouldn't get into their eyes and mouths. Just before they got back on the horses, Calista and Lisa saw something moving in the sand and pointed at it. It got bigger and bigger as it moved toward them.

Four sand demons rose out of the sand and glared at them, grinding their teeth. The demons jumped back into the sand and swam toward them; everybody jumped back onto the horses and rode away from the demons. The demons jumped out of the sand again in front of them, scaring the horses. The horses reared up wildly and knocked the riders to the ground. They got up and began fighting the demons.

A puff of black smoke appeared, and Supay rose out of the sand to join the sand demons in battle. Phil shot his mini stake cannon at a demon. The demon sizzled and burned before turning into ashes. Devon took the hush hound, aimed it at another demon, and shot it, causing that demon to disintegrate as well. Sand slowly began to whip around in the air, and a sandstorm started around them. As the storm picked up in intensity, the horses dropped onto their knees. The others huddled together and balled up. Supay and the other demons continued to try to fight.

When the sandstorm finally ended, the Valley of the Lost was shimmering with sand and there was nothing in sight. Seconds later, they slowly dug themselves out of a huge mound of sand and dusted themselves off. The black smoke appeared again, and Supay and the other demons rose up again and started fighting once more. One of the demons grabbed a royal guard by the neck and raised him off the ground; the demon tightened its grip around the guard's neck. The guard's head popped off his body, and his body fell to the sandy ground.

Lord Devon turned around, saw his guard's headless body on the ground, and let out a long scream. Devon shoved a silver stake into the chest of the demon and twisted it. The demon wailed in agony and fell to the ground. Supay saw what happened and quickly disappeared in a cloud of smoke.

"How the hell did Supay get here?" Phil asked.

"Angels and demons can move through time and space naturally whenever they want," Ruth answered.

"How do you know that?" Phil asked.

"Muggsy and I did some research when we learned about Azazelbog and Supay," Ruth replied.

"We should pay our respects to the fallen," Lord Devon said as tears rolled down his cheeks.

They all knelt down, made the sign of the cross on their chests, and bowed their heads. Lord Devon wrapped the body in a cloth and tied it to a horse; they got back on the horses and rode away. As they were riding, Muggsy pointed west, and they followed that direction. They crossed another deep, vast sand plateau and suddenly stopped in front of a giant boulder.

"The *X* marks the spot," Muggsy said.

"Now what?" Calista asked.

"Now we dig," Muggsy answered.

Muggsy threw a spade to each of the others, and they all began to dig. Beads of sweat poured down their bodies as the sun beat down on them. An hour later, they hit something solid. Muggsy dusted the sand away, revealing solid stone ground. On the ground was a large knob, and on the knob was a symbol, the same symbol that was etched on the Warriors of Raw armor.

"I have an idea," Joseph said.

He took off the armor and placed it over the etching on the knob. The stone knob revolved three times and began to crumble away. Just as the armor began to fall, Joseph caught it and put it back on; the stone floor crumbled away, revealing a perfectly circular hole. Brandon tied a rope to one of the horse's saddles and threw the other end into the hole.

"Lord Devon, you and the guards wait here and stand watch," Muggsy said. "Just shout if those demons return."

The others took hold of the rope and went down into the hole one by one. It led to a huge, endless cavern that was cooler than the desert. They finally reached the end of the ropes and jumped down to the ground. In the far corner of the cavern was a stone door in the wall. Right next to the stone door was an oddly shaped stone protruding from outside of the wall; Joseph pushed the stone and the door opened. They walked through a narrow hall that led them into a smaller chamber; salt was sprinkled all around the chamber. Again, the symbol on the Warriors of Raw armor was carved into the wall. Joseph took off the armor again, covered the symbol, and twisted it; a small chunk of the wall opened, revealing a hole. Inside the hole was a dusty, old wooden crate.

Phil broke the crate open to expose something wrapped up in a cloth and tied; it was surrounded by salt. He untied it to reveal the

Dagger of Destiny. The dagger was old and long, and etched in the blade were the words IN GOD WE TRUST. It began shining brightly. They wrapped the dagger up again and walked back to the rope. They took turns holding tightly to the rope, and the guards and Devon pulled each of them up.

"Did any more demons attack?" Phil asked.

"We saw a demon swimming in the sand, but it did not attack," Devon replied. "May I see the Dagger of Destiny?"

Muggsy unwrapped the dagger and handed it to Lord Devon. He stared at it in amazement.

"I thought I would never see this in my lifetime," Devon solemnly said. "You know something? This is indeed special."

"Don't worry—we'll take good care of it," Phil said.

They jumped on their horses and rode away. A demon followed them in the sand for miles without their knowing, and a couple of hours later, the Valley of the Lost ended and the sand demon disappeared. It took them almost two days to get back.

"We are going to have a burial ceremony for the fallen guard, and we would appreciate it if you would attend," Lord Devon said.

"We'll definitely come pay our respects," Muggsy said.

"Then we will see you later this evening," Devon said.

Lord Devon and the guards got back onto their horses and left. The kids let the animals out and fed them. Cheats heard them, so he crept outside and began licking them. Brandon and Isaiah fed Cheats and the kids continued playing with him. Then they went to rest for a while. At five o'clock, they got up, Liza put the farm animals away, and they all got ready for the burial.

When they got to the castle, they were escorted into the throne room. People were lining up to view the guard's body. They bowed their heads in front of the oaken box and then went to sit in the back. A while later, when everyone was done viewing the body, four guards grabbed the sides of the wooden box, lifted it, and walked down the aisle, everyone following. When they reached the burial yard, they placed the wooden box in a hole. Monks prayed over the hole and placed wooden planks on top, lighting them. They all began singing funeral hymns. Once the fire died down, the monks and guards covered the hole with a huge boulder. An hour later, Lord Devon bid everyone farewell.

When they got back to the farm, they put the horses back into the stables, fed Cheats, and went to sleep. In the morning, they all woke up at the same time and washed up for breakfast. They let out the farm animals and ate breakfast. When they were done eating, Lisa, Phil, and Calista went to the stream and began skipping pebbles; a little later, Muggsy came and joined them. Soon they were all splashing around in the stream.

It grew cooler, so they got out of the water, went back to the farm, and dried off. When they were done changing, Muggsy, Ruth, and the kids started to get their things packed up. Just as they were finishing, Lillian and Daniel rode up in a wagon.

"We wanted to see you before you go," Lillian said.

Daniel gave Brandon a big hug and kissed him.

"Tell your father what you wanted to tell him," Lillian said.

"I love you, Father, and I am going to miss you," Daniel said.

Brandon held Daniel even tighter. "I am going to miss you so much, son," Brandon said.

Lisa took a diary out of her bag and went outside to look at the book. A couple of minutes later, Anna came out and joined Lisa.

"What are you doing out here by yourself, dear?" Anna asked.

"Well, while I was here, I wanted to meet my great-great-great-great-grandfather," Lisa said.

"What was his name?" Anna asked.

"His name was Linus Mathais," Lisa replied.

"My father's name was Linus Mathais," Anna said. "You know what that means?"

"Yes, I came from your bloodline. I'm part of your family," Lisa said.

The two embraced warmly before going back inside and joining in the conversation the others were having.

"If you need any help from the Warriors of Raw in the war against Azazelbog and Supay, just let us know and we will be there," Joseph said.

"Thank you so much—and we will," Muggsy said.

"Do you really think that there is going to be a war between good and evil?" Liza asked.

"We are hoping it doesn't escalate into a war, but we have to do anything to stop these demons," Phil said as tears rolled down his cheeks.

"What is wrong, dear?" Anna asked.

"Azazelbog took over Alex's body," Phil replied sadly.

"Oh, honey, do not worry. We will destroy this Azazelbog and bring Alex's soul to peace," Liza said.

"Do you want something to eat before you leave?" Anna asked.

"No, we are okay," Ruth said, and the others agreed.

A little later, Muggsy took the radio and connected to Ryan in the future to prepare the portal for their return. Muggsy then turned off the radio, and they all went outside and played with Cheats. Cheats began licking Daniel and playing with him as if they had been friends for a lifetime.

After some time, Lord Devon and two royal guards came riding down the field on their horses. They jumped down from their horses and walked over to them. Devon shook all their hands and smiled at them. He started petting Cheats, who licked Lord Devon.

"I came here to say thank you for coming to the burial of my fallen guard," Devon said.

"It's no problem. He gave his life to help us," Muggsy said.

"If you need any assistance in the fight against these demons, just let me know and I will be there," Devon said.

"Thank you," Phil said.

"No problem. I must go; the queen and I are meeting foreign royalty in a while."

Devon and the guards got back onto their horses and rode away. Muggsy, the kids, and Ruth grabbed their bags and weapons and went back outside to the field, followed by those they would be leaving behind.

"When is Ryan going to open the portal?" Ruth asked.

"He said in an hour, and that was about forty-five minutes ago," Muggsy said.

Static bellowed from the radio and Ryan's voice filled the air. "The portal will open in two minutes," he said.

"Okay," Muggsy called into the radio.

Muggsy turned off the radio. Just then, a gust of wind blew around, nearly knocking them over, and electricity shot between two trees. The electricity formed into a circle, and the jellied center formed. Brandon embraced Lillian and Daniel and kissed them.

"I will always love you, son, and I will be back soon to see you," Brandon said. He turned to Lillian. "I will come and visit as soon as this is over."

Ruth, the kids, and Muggsy hugged everyone and bid them farewell. They walked into the portal, and it closed behind them.

CHAPTER 9

The Guardians of Souls and The Techno-Organic

When they got to the Quest Inc. headquarters it was dark and eerily quiet. They were soaked in the liquid jelly; they grabbed some towels off the conference table and cleaned themselves off. They then got into the lift and went up to Muggsy's office. Phil unlatched the lift gate and they got off. They found Lynda, Pat, and Toby talking in the office.

"Did you get the Spear of Destiny?" Pat asked.

"You mean the Dagger of Destiny. And yes, we did," Phil answered.

Muggsy took the dagger out, unwrapped it, and showed it to them.

"This is the greatest historical artifact in all of history, you know," Toby said.

"Yes, that is why we have to protect it with our lives," Ruth said.

"What's happened since we've been gone?" Muggsy asked.

"Well, it's been really quiet. There's no activity on Azazelbog's end," Lynda said.

Ryan entered the office and shook everybody's hand. They all took seats.

"I'm sorry I wasn't there when you came back," Ryan said. "Luca and I were working on a prototype for a new Quest Inc. suit, so we had to get a few things."

"Are you finished with the prototype yet? Can we see it?" Muggsy asked.

"No, not yet. But we're almost done working on it," Ryan answered.

"How are Gina, Denise, Becky, and Zoe doing?" Muggsy asked. "Have they proven they're trustworthiness and loyalty to Quest Inc.?"

"It seems they have," Lynda said.

"Hold on. You mean you still do not trust them?" Ruth asked, sounding disturbed.

"I'm sorry, but no, I didn't. You could trust them, but I didn't know if I could," Muggsy said.

"I just thought the trust you had in me would be enough to trust them," Ruth said sadly.

"All I can do now is apologize to you," Muggsy said.

"Okay, then I guess I forgive you," Ruth said.

"So, Ryan, is that protective case ready for the dagger?"

"Yes, it's ready. I made it for a full-size spear, but I think it will work all the same. It'll protect against any bullet or knife. But the only thing that it doesn't protect from is spells or demon powers."

"Do not worry about the coven and I will place protective spells on the case," Ruth said.

Ruth made a phone call, and moments later, she, Ryan, and Muggsy got into the lift and it slowly descended. Toby, Lynda, and Pat stayed in the office and talked. A little later, the doorbell rang, and Zoe, Gina, Becky, and Denise soon came into the office, greeted them, and they all sat down and talked. The coven eventually got up and went down to the Quest Inc. headquarters.

Phil, Isaiah, and Brandon went up to the boys' dorm, changed their clothes, and unpacked their bags. When they were done unpacking, they sat around and talked. The cuckoo clock chimed seven o'clock, and Stanchie and Melissa came into the dorm and joined in the conversation.

"Guess what, Phil," Stanchie said.

"What?" Phil asked.

"Look what Zack and Matt gave us," Melissa said, and they held out their hands.

On both of their middle fingers were rings with birthstones in them.

"When did they give them to you?" Phil asked.

"We went to the mall yesterday, and they got these for us. They said they promise to be with us forever," Stanchie replied.

"I'm sorry to be such a downer, but nothing lasts forever," Phil said.

"I'm sorry you feel like that," Calista said as she entered the room. She sat down and joined them in the conversation.

Doris then joined them in the dorm room. "How is everything?" she asked.

"Everything is fine. We retrieved the Dagger of Destiny," Phil replied.

"What do you mean, 'dagger'?" Doris asked.

Phil and Isaiah explained to Doris how the spear became a dagger.

"I'd better go finish getting dinner ready," Doris said. "And make sure you come and eat. Tonight is mac and cheese night."

Doris left the room, and the kids headed to the game room to play pool. Around seven thirty, everybody went to the dining room for dinner. When Phil was done eating, he took his dishes to the kitchen and headed to the boys' dorm. As the other boys filled the room, Phil crawled into his bed and went to sleep.

In the morning, once he'd had breakfast, Phil went to the living room, turned on the television, and watched MTV. He spent some time talking with a group of boys who came into the room. When they left, Phil continued to watch TV. After an hour or so, Calista, Lisa, and Stanchie came into the living room, and the three of them talked. They slowly made their way outside to the backyard and began playing basketball.

There was suddenly the sound of the telephone ringing. A girl stuck her head out the doorway and called Stanchie. She hurried inside. A few minutes later, Stanchie returned.

"Zack and Matt want Melissa and me to go to the park. Do you want to come with us?"

"That would be cool, but we should check with Muggsy," Phil said.

"Don't worry. I asked Muggsy, and she said it's okay," Stanchie said.

"Okay, then let me just go and get my skateboard," Phil said.

Phil went up to the boys' dorm, got his skateboard, and met the others in the den. They quickly left the house, and Phil closed the door behind them. When they got to the park, the boys started to shred.

"Did you see the rings we got Stanchie and Melissa?" Matt asked.

"Do you mind if I ask you something? How could you promise Stanchie and Melissa *forever* if you can't promise them *tomorrow?*" Phil asked.

"Because we really care about them." Zack said. "Dude, please stop being a killjoy."

"I'm sorry. Let's just shred," Phil said.

A little while later, the boys stopped shredding, and they all went to the handball courts and played handball. As the day drew on, people slowly began to clear out of the park until they were the only ones left. Phil, Zack, and Matt grabbed their decks and they left the park. On their way home, a strange heavy wind began blowing, nearly knocking them over.

Then a fiery hole burned through the street, and Azazelbog, Supay, and two other demons rose out of the ground and began to fight them. One of the demons grabbed Melissa and Calista and threw them; the girls hit a tree and fell to the ground with a thud. Azazelbog seized Phil's neck and lifted him up, but a knife suddenly pierced Azazelbog in the back. He shrieked in agony and fell to his knees. Azazelbog then grinned evilly, pulled the knife out of his back, and started to laugh. The knife wound quickly began sizzling and burning, and then it disappeared.

He abruptly turned around and frowned madly, for there were three people standing behind them. They were wearing sack-looking clothing, and stitched into the chests of their clothing was a picture of an angel killing a demon. They were armed with crossbows and swords.

"What the hell are you doing here?" Azazelbog snarled loudly.

"We are here to stop you devil boy," one of the men called out.

"That's what you think!" Azazelbog snarled.

He slapped his hands together, and a fireball shot out of his hands and flew toward the three people. The three of them jumped out of the way, and the fireball hit a tree, engulfing it in flames. Azazelbog and Supay shrieked with an earth-shattering tone.

"Cover your ears, children!" one of the warriors called out.

They all covered their ears with their hands as a shockwave shot through the air, hitting two houses and shattering the windows.

"Don't worry—we'll get even, and we'll kill all you fleshlings!" Azazelbog snarled.

Seconds later, a fiery hole appeared again, swallowing Azazelbog, Supay, and the other demons. The hole closed behind them.

"We will accompany you children home," one of the warriors said.

"Thank you," Isaiah said.

Phil, Matt, and Zack retrieved their broken skateboards, and they all walked down the street. There was total silence between them as they walked; it was so quiet that they could hear the insects chirping. The warriors circled around the children with their weapons at the ready in case the demons returned. They finally got to the orphanage and walked up the stoop. Phil pressed the doorbell, and Muggsy opened the door and stared at the warriors.

"We just wanted to accompany these children home because we saw that they were in trouble," the female warrior said.

"Thanks for bring them home," Muggsy said. "Kids, get inside."

The children went inside, and Muggsy started to close the door, but one of the warriors held the door open.

"We would like to speak to the maiden Muggsy," one of the warriors said.

"I'm Muggsy, and there's no need to call me *maiden*. Now, what do you need?"

"We were sent here to join Quest Inc. in its battle against Azazelbog and Supay," one of the warriors said. "I am Joshua, this is Steffany, and that is Joanna. We are the Guardians of Souls. We were sent here by the head of the church."

"How do you know that we are Quest Inc.—and how can we trust you?" Muggsy asked.

"We have been observing your activities for a couple of days now, and if you do not trust us, just contact the head of the church," Joanna said.

"I'm going to check your story out, but if I don't like what I hear, I'm not going to be happy." Muggsy turned around. "Doris, come here for a second," she called out.

"Will you watch these characters while I make a call?" Muggsy asked when she arrived.

"Of course I will," Doris replied.

As Muggsy walked away, Doris stared at the warriors. Muggsy returned a few minutes later, and Doris went back inside again.

"Okay, I made a few calls, and your story checks out. But I still find it creepy that you were checking us out for days without our knowing," Muggsy said.

"We are sorry. We just had to make sure you were Quest Inc.," Steffany said.

"What are the Guardians of Souls?" Muggsy asked.

"We will explain that to you, but first may we come in?" Johanna asked.

"Oh, yes, come in," Muggsy said.

The Guardians of Souls walked into the orphanage, Muggsy closed the door behind them, and they went to Muggsy's office, where she sat down at her desk.

"Now, what is the Guardians of Souls, exactly?" Muggsy asked.

"We are a group of immortals brought together by the hand of God to stop evil from taking over the world," Steffany explained.

"How were you brought together to become the Guardians of Souls, and how are you immortal?" Muggsy asked.

"Well, I was the unknown pope of the fifteenth century, and Steffany was the head of the Sisters of the Vatican at that time. We both were on a mission for the church when Johanna ended up saving our lives, and from then on we were inseparable," Joshua explained. "On that same mission, the three of us were at the point of death when we drank from the Chalice of Youth."

"But why were you called to help us?" Muggsy asked.

"This fight between good and evil, this fight between the human world and Azazelbog and the demons, will become a huge war." Johanna said. "Azazelbog will have a multitude of demons and the evil undead on his side. You will have to have more people on your forces."

"You are welcome to fight with us in this war, but there is no room to stay with us," Muggsy said. "I'll call one of my friends and see if you can stay with him."

"Thank you for that," Joshua said.

Muggsy called Toby, and then she told them, "My friend Toby said you can stay with him. We're about to eat dinner, so you can eat with us."

They left the office and went to the dining room. While they were eating, the doorbell rang, and Muggsy left to answer it. She soon returned with Toby. He grabbed a plate of food, and he and

Muggsy sat down together. After dinner, the guests left for the night, and everyone in the orphanage went to bed.

The next morning when everyone was done eating breakfast, Phil collected all the dirty dishes and went into the kitchen to wash them. When he was done, he went to the den. A girl came into the room and began talking to Phil. The girl left awhile later, leaving the den quiet again. When Phil heard whispering in the hallway, he crept to the doorway and put his ear to the door.

"Do you really think this is going to work?" Ryan asked.

"I think it will," Luca answered.

"But when we fuse the techno-organic bio skin to the new Q.I. suits, will the wearer be okay?"

"To my race's knowledge, it will be fine, and that is why I'm going to test it out on myself," Luca replied.

They walked into Muggsy's office, and Phil heard the lift slowly descend. Phil sat down again, and thoughts quickly raced through his head. What were Ryan and Luca working on? And could what they were working on really help in the fight against Azazelbog and Supay? He went upstairs to the dorm, changed into shorts and a T-shirt, and went to the backyard to play basketball alone.

He eventually lost track of time as the hot air slowly cooled down. The day became darker and darker. Muggsy stuck her head out of the doorway and called Phil in for dinner. After dinner, he went up to the boys' dorm and changed into sweatpants and a T-shirt. Thoughts about Ryan and Luca's conversation were still running through his head.

He walked over to his bed and lay down with a book in hand. As he was reading, he didn't notice the other boys slowly filling the room. That night, Phil fell asleep with the opened book on his chest.

The following morning, he woke up refreshed. He washed up for breakfast and headed to the first-floor landing; however, Muggsy stopped him.

"Ryan and Luca have to show us something," Muggsy said. They went to the headquarters to find Ryan and Luca waiting for them.

"This is the prototype for the new techno-organic Q.I. suits," Ryan said. He pulled a sheet off the conference table to reveal the suit. It was made of the same hard rubber like the suits they had now. Embedded in the suit and covering it were computer circuits and wiring. On top of the wiring and computer circuits was natural jellied webbing covering the suit. Next to the suit was a helmet that resembled a motorcycle sports helmet, but it was thinner material.

"Luca will put the suit on and show you how it works," Ryan said.

"What do you mean, 'how it works'?" Muggsy asked.

"You'll see," Ryan replied.

Luca put on the new suit and locked the helmet into place on top of the suit. "The suit changes into the form of any organic-based life form you can think of," Luca began to explain. "You and the suit will also have the strength and the agility of that life-form."

The jellied webbing began to glow, and the suit slowly started to change. The helmet changed into a lion's head; the body of the suit changed into muscles. Luca climbed onto the wall and then jumped from wall to wall. He then jumped down onto the ground, picked up a metal chair, and crushed it into a ball. A second later, when the suit changed back to normal, Luca unlocked the helmet and took it off.

"Okay, but does this suit have any problems with it?" Muggsy asked.

"There are no kinks in the suit," Luca answered quickly. "The only thing is that the transformations only last for an hour. Then it has to recharge for five minutes before the next transformation."

"Can you lengthen the transformation time?" Muggsy asked.

"I can try, but I can't make any promises," Luca replied.

Muggsy and Phil were about to leave when Luca stopped them. "I have to show you something else," Luca said. "But we will have to go outside so I can demonstrate it."

Luca picked up a small metal box, and the four of them left headquarters and went to the backyard. Luca opened the box and took out two objects that looked similar to grenades. The next-door neighbor's dog started jumping up and down and barking at them. Luca threw one of the grenades toward the dog. It blew up, and roots started growing out of the exploded grenade. The roots quickly grabbed hold of the dog, covering its entire body and twisting it until it tore in half.

Luca threw the other grenade-looking object, and it blew up and turned into a plant-based techno-organic humanoid. The humanoid looked mostly plant based, although it did have electric wire veins pulsing through its body.

"The first one is techno-organic exploding sprouts," Luca said. "The second is called the vegetating humanoid."

"But you just killed the neighbors' dog."

"I'm truly sorry for doing that. I will replace it for them," Luca replied.

"I do have to admit those are affective," Muggsy said. "We saw what the Techno-Organic Exploding Sprouts does, but what can the Vegetating Humanoid do?"

"It is fully combat ready. Let me demonstrate," Luca said.

Luca grabbed a wooden staff, and he and the vegetating humanoid got into battle stance and started to fight. Luca took the staff and began hitting the humanoid, and it began blocking the strikes. All of a sudden, the humanoid jumped into the air and kicked Luca in the chest and landed on its feet.

"Battle ended," Luca called out, and the humanoid froze again. "See, it is fully mobile and battle ready."

The four of them went back inside, leaving the Vegetating Humanoid frozen in suspended animation. Luca, Muggsy, Phil, and Ryan went back to Q.I. headquarters A little later, they went to the dining room for dinner. When Phil was done eating, he went up to the boys' dorm and went to sleep.

The next morning when he was finished with breakfast, Phil went up to the girls' dorm to hang out and talk with Lisa and Calista. A few minutes later, Isaiah, Madison, and Brandon came into the dorm and joined them. The six of them left quite a while later to go hang out in the warm summer air.

While Muggsy and Luca were talking to each other in in the Quest Inc. headquarters, the lift came down and Lynda and Pat entered the room.

"We've got intel from Mr. and Mrs. Matthews," Lynda said, "There's been a lot of movement in the cemetery. Azazelbog is gathering more and more forces."

"Luca, did you change the timing of the transformation in the new techno-organic Q.I. suits?" Muggsy asked.

"Yes, I did. Now the transformation time lasts an hour and a half, but it still takes five minutes to recharge."

The kids were hanging out in the game room when footsteps echoed through the hallway, and Lynda and Pat stuck their heads into the game room.

"How are you doing, my pigeons?" Lynda asked them as she and Pat entered the room.

"Oh my gosh, we haven't seen you in a while!" Lisa quickly exclaimed. "How are you?"

"Everything is good, my dears," Pat replied. "Some people came to see you."

Pat's and Lynda's husbands and Pat's daughters walked into the room. "Guess what! We just joined Q.I.," Lynda and Pat's families said.

"We're really happy you joined, but are you sure you want to do it now?" Phil asked worriedly. "We're working on a huge mission."

"And we'll be ready for it," Pat's and Lynda's husbands said together.

Later that night, Phil crawled into his bed and tried to sleep. During the night, he was restless, tossing and turning and unable to sleep.

Chapter 10

The Betrayals

When Phil woke up from the blinding light of the sun, he still felt sleepy. He got ready for the day and went downstairs. When he was done with breakfast, he went out to the backyard and hung out with Isaiah and Brandon. The morning passed quickly, and around one o'clock, they went to Muggsy's office. Phil knocked on the door, and they entered. Muggsy was talking on the phone, so they sat down and waited until she was done. When she hung up, they asked if they and the girls could go to the park, and she told them it was okay.

The boys quickly left the room and went up to the girls' dorm. They all left the orphanage a short time later. When they met Zack and Matt at the park, Zack kissed Melissa and Matt kissed Stanchie. The boys started skating, and the girls sat on the swings and talked. An hour later, the boys skated over to the girls and began pushing them on the swings.

At four o'clock, they left the park, and when they got to the orphanage, Phil noted that it was oddly quiet. But then a noisy group of boys suddenly ran out of the dining room and up the stairs. Muggsy called them from her office, and they went down to the Q.I. headquarters.

In the cemetery, right outside the catacombs, was a group of about one hundred of Azazelbog's followers. A big shadow abruptly appeared in the entrance, and a minute later, Supay and Azazelbog walked out of the catacombs. They threw their arms into the air, and their followers began chanting their names. The goth girl walked up to Azazelbog, bowed down in front of him, stood and whispered into his ear, and walked away.

Azazelbog took Supay aside and stared into his eyes. "Some of our followers have informed me that you're going to try to betray me by telling my father that I'm trying to take over this world!" Azazelbog hissed. "Is this true?"

"I assure you I'm doing no such thing!" Supay exclaimed.

"You know that if my father finds out, he'll drag me back to hell," Azazelbog snarled.

"Fine, you want to know the truth? I was planning to tell your father," Supay quickly snarled back. "You don't deserve to possess this world."

"You will pay for trying to betray me! I'm going to cast you so far back into hell that my father and no other thing will find you."

The ground of the graveyard began shaking, and a huge hole ripped through the ground of the catacombs. Azazelbog took Supay by the neck and threw him into the wall. He picked Supay up by the neck again while grabbing his chest. Supay screamed in agony as Azazelbog pulled Supay's demon form out of the human body. Supay's demon form struggled to break free from Azazelbog's grasps, but to no avail. Azazelbog started chanting and threw Supay into the hole, which closed up behind him.

"The fleshling is still alive. Bring him to me. He can still prove to be useful," Azazelbog called out.

His followers dragged Jeremy's tired worn-out body into the abandoned house and shackled him up to a wall. Azazelbog's eyes glowed yellow, and he began hollering in hunger.

The kids in the orphanage were hanging out in the game room. Phil got up off the sofa and went to the boys' dorm, took a book off his dresser, and began reading on his bed. The afternoon slowly went by, turning into night. When Doris called everyone for dinner, Phil put down the book and went down to the dining room. When Phil was done eating he went back to the dorm and went to sleep.

In the morning, everybody woke up and got ready for the day. When Phil was done getting ready, he went to the girls' dorm and hung out with Lisa, Madison, and Calista. After they were done with breakfast, they went to the backyard and splashed around in the pool for a while. After they went back inside, the girls went to their dorm and Phil went to the den to watch TV. As he settled on the sofa, he heard footsteps and then the sound of the lift.

If there was nothing going on with Quest Inc. today, then who was going to the headquarters? He wondered. He ran to Muggsy's office, but the lift had already descended.

In the Q.I. headquarters, the lift gate opened and Ruth and the other coven members walked out of it. They started placing protective spells all around the headquarters as they talked.

"Muggsy is losing her trust in the coven," Ruth said.

"But why is that?" Becky asked.

"I am not sure, but I just thought you four should know," Ruth said as the lift came down again "We will talk later."

The lift stopped, and Phil walked into the large room. "Hey, what are you doing here?" Phil asked them.

"We're placing protection spells, just in case Azazelbog tries to enter headquarters again," Zoe answered.

"So how are things going with the coven?" Phil asked.

"Everything's going well," Gina replied. "Guess what! We conjured up a nature spirit."

"That sounds really cool," Phil said.

He bid them farewell and quickly left headquarters, going to his dorm and playing a video game on the computer. The rest of the day slowly drew on. What felt like hours were only minutes. Around ten o'clock, Phil went to sleep.

The rest of the week quickly flew by, and the following Tuesday, things went awry with Quest Inc. Tensions were high between the coven and Muggsy because she was losing trust in them.

Phil and Calista came down for breakfast. While they were eating, they heard Becky and Zoe arguing with Muggsy in the hallway. As the three of them entered the dining room, they stopped arguing. Although they got their food and sat down to eat, the ice-cold silence between Muggsy, Zoe and Becky cut through the air like a knife.

After eating, Phil and Calista went up to the game room and played pool, and a couple of minutes later, Isaiah and Brandon came and joined the game. Later in the day, Muggsy took the younger children of the orphanage to the park. Around six o'clock, they returned to the orphanage. Muggsy went to her office.

After some time Doris called everybody for dinner. When Phil was finished eating, he and the girls went to the backyard and hung out. At ten o'clock, they went back inside. Calista kissed

Phil on the cheek, and they went to their respective dorms. Phil changed into shorts and a tank top and went to sleep.

The following morning when he woke up, he saw that all the other boys were still in bed, so he quietly got ready and crept out of the dorm. The orphanage was so quiet and peaceful since everyone was still sleeping. He went to the backyard, grabbed a basketball, and started shooting hoops. A little while later, Brandon came outside and joined him. At nine o'clock, they went back inside and had breakfast.

"There is so much tension in Quest Inc. that something is going to give," Brandon said after swallowing a bite of food. "I do not even understand why Muggsy does not trust the coven."

"I know. That whole thing between them is just dumb," Phil added.

Lisa, Calista, and Madison sat down next to them and joined in the conversation. When they were done eating, they took their dishes to the kitchen and left the dining room. They went up to the game room and played pool and video games. Around noon, the girls bid farewell to Phil and left the room.

A few minutes later, Phil turned off the video game console and left the room. As he walked downstairs, he heard some commotion on the first floor. It was coming from Muggsy's office. She was yelling at someone on the phone.

The lift ascended, and the coven ran out.

"Who do you think you are talking to me like that!" Becky exclaimed.

"No, who do you think you are raising your voice at me!" Muggsy yelled back.

"Calm down, Becky," Zoe said as she looked at Muggsy. "We're sorry about that."

"I will not calm down. The coven has done nothing wrong to Muggsy or Quest Inc. to lose faith in us."

Suddenly, there was silence.

"Yeah, I thought so—no answer. I'm tired of this crap. I'm outta here!" Becky exclaimed to Muggsy. She turned to Ruth, Zoe, and Gina. "Are you coming with me?"

The three of them just looked at her with sad looks on their faces.

"Now I know that I'm rolling alone," Becky said. She stormed out of the office.

"We should go after her," Ruth said.

"Don't worry—she'll come back after she calms down," Muggsy said.

Becky stormed out of the orphanage and walked to the bus stop. When the bus came, Becky got on and sat in the back. The bus eventually stopped in front of Flushing Cemetery. Becky got off the bus, walked into the cemetery, and started looking for Azazelbog. She found a secret underground passageway to the catacombs and began calling him.

"Come over here now, Azazelbog, I have to talk to you!"

Azazelbog appeared with fire dancing around him. He slapped Becky in the face, and she flew into a wall, falling with a thud. He glided over to her and picked her up by the neck. "You are part of Quest Inc.," Azazelbog hissed. "How dare you summon me, fleshling?"

"I've split from Quest Inc. I'm sick and tired of not being trusted," Becky said. "Can you help me?"

He stared into her eyes and waved his left hand over her, smirking evilly.

"I feel such power coursing through your body. I could use you in my army," Azazelbog said. "Are you ready to denounce good and join the dark side?"

"Yes, I am," Becky replied.

Azazelbog held Becky's hands and began laughing; Becky's energy slowly started draining as wind blew around them.

It was dinnertime at the orphanage; however, it was quiet in the dining room. By this point, everyone knew Becky had left the coven. *Things have felt strange with the coven ever since Becky left*, Phil thought. When they were done eating, Phil and Calista went to the den and began talking. After some time, Lisa came into the room. She said good night to Phil, and she and Calista left the den.

After a couple of days passed, things at the orphanage and Quest Inc. calmed down. It was business as usual, and Muggsy held a Q.I. meeting to show the other members the new techno-organic suit. Right after the meeting, Muggsy and Toby went back to the office. A while later, Mr. and Mrs. Matthews came out of Muggsy's office and left the orphanage. Pat and Lynda went out to the backyard and talked with Phil.

Late the next morning, Muggsy took Phil aside. "I was going to have a barbecue tonight. Will you call the Matthews family and Ryan?" Muggsy asked.

"I'm going to meet Zack and Matt at the park later, so I'll tell them," Phil replied. "But isn't Ryan down in headquarters?"

"No. He and Luca were working double time to make more of the new techno-organic suites, so I told them to take a break."

"Okay, I'll call Ryan," Phil said.

He went upstairs to the boys' dorm and called Ryan. A couple of minutes later, he hung up the telephone, grabbed his new skateboard, and went back to the backyard.

"Where are Stanchie and Melissa?" Phil asked Calista and Lisa.

"They're getting ready for Matt and Zack," Lisa answered.

"Where are Isaiah and Brandon?" asked Phil.

"They went to the store with Doris. We will meet you at the park later," Madison replied.

A couple of minutes later Stanchie and Melissa came out. After saying good-bye to Madison and Phil, the girls walked down the walkway and slowly out of sight. When they got to the park, Zack and Matt were sitting talking to a group of boys. Melissa and Stanchie went over to Matt and Zack and kissed them, also rubbing their backs. A few minutes later Isaiah, Madison and Brandon arrived. The boys took their skateboards and started shredding, and the girls sat and talked.

It was six o'clock when they left the park and headed to the orphanage. The barbecue was already under way. There were mouthwatering smells of grilled shrimp, burgers, and hot dogs. Everyone was dancing and talking as music filled the air.

Doris came over to them. "Come and have something to eat," Doris said. She looked at Phil. "Don't worry—I made some grilled mushroom and peppers and veggie burgers for you."

They got plates and cups and filled them with food and drinks. A little later, Lynda and Pat approached them.

"How are you kids doing?" Lynda asked.

"We're good," Stanchie replied. "What are you doing here?"

"Muggsy told us to come," Pat answered.

"We were scouting around in the cemetery, and we found out that Azazelbog sent Supay back to hell because he was trying to betray him," Lynda told them. "The bad thing is that they're still holding Jeremy. We tried to free him, but Azazelbog's followers caught us and stopped us."

"Oh my gosh, are you two okay?" Phil asked.

"We're fine," Pat said. "Just a couple of scrapes. Luckily Pete and Jay were there."

Pete and Jay came over to them; they had scars on their arms and down their faces.

"Oh my gosh, look at you two. Pat and Lynda said you were okay," Calista said.

"Don't worry. They're just a couple of scars," Pete said.

"I don't want you to be in Quest Inc. anymore!" Phil exclaimed.

"Look, we all knew what we were getting into when we joined Quest Inc.," Jay said.

There was total silence between them, and then Pete said, "I'm sorry you feel that way, but we're staying in Quest Inc."

Lynda, Jay, Pat, and Pete hugged Phil and walked away.

CHAPTER 11

The Death of Friends

The barbecue went on all evening, and the beat of the music filled the air. Some kids were splashing around in the pool; others were dancing. Around ten o'clock, Muggsy turned off the music, and she and Doris began cleaning up. The Matthews family said good night to everyone and left. Pat, Jay, Lynda, and Pete stayed behind to help clean up while the kids went up to the dorms and changed for bed. Fifteen minutes later, Lynda and Pat came inside, said good night to the kids, and left. Phil crawled into his bed and went to sleep.

The next morning, while Phil was getting ready for the day, he stared at the dorm room calendar with a puzzled look on his face. *This summer went by quickly*, he thought.

The morning was uneventful, as it was quiet and calm. When afternoon finally came, Calista and Phil were still hanging around outside; Isaiah, Madison, and Brandon came outside and joined them. They got into the pool and played water volleyball.

At Flushing Cemetery, it was very quiet, so quiet that one could hear birds chirping from across the cemetery. The silence was broken when there was loud chanting from Azazelbog's followers. Except for Becky, his followers' human body forms began to change. Their teeth became sharp and started rotting. Their nails got longer and sharper, and their skin became wrinkled and scaly. Azazelbog emerged from the catacombs with blood on his lips. His long snakelike tongue wrapped around his lips and licked the blood off. Azazelbog threw his arms up into the air, and his followers chanted even louder.

"It's my time to rule this world; it's time for evil to finally be in charge!" Azazelbog exclaimed. "The prophecy says that the son of the highest evil will rule in the land near the sea where two large brotherly twins stood and fell. The time for evil to rule is in the thousandth year after the first thousand years, when the sun and all the planets are in line and when the sun and moon are as red as blood."

His followers cheered and chanted even louder. Becky and one of the other followers dragged out Jeremy's body and chained him up to a large tombstone.

"I'm going to bring forth a Deval demon to inhabit this fleshling body. They are large and dumb but very loyal," Azazelbog said. "She definitely will not betray me."

Azazelbog started chanting, and a large crack ripped through the ground. The crack opened up a little wider, turning into a huge hole. A demon suddenly rose out of the hole; it was large, with bat-like wings and a long snout. The demon began to snarl, and it slowly entered Jeremy's body. Jeremy started screaming in agony as his whole body began to expand and writhe. Seconds later, his mouth shut and his eyes began to glow. The Deval snarled and grunted, and drool dripped down its mouth. Lava shot out of the hole and immediately dried up and hardened, covering the hole.

The following morning in the orphanage, Phil went to the girls' dorm and walked with Calista and Lisa down to the dining room. When they were finished eating, the three of them went outside. A little while later, Isaiah, Madison, Brandon, Melissa, and Stanchie joined them. Ryan soon came out and grabbed a basketball.

"You want to shoot some hoops?" Ryan asked.

"That would be cool," Phil replied.

The boys and girls split up into two teams, and they started playing ball. When the game was over, they collapsed, their clothes drenched in sweat.

"You know we guys let you win?" Ryan asked.

"Yeah, you guys keep thinking that," Calista laughed.

"Are you and Luca done making all the new techno-organic Quest Inc. suits?" Lisa asked.

"No, not really. We've only completed twenty of them," Ryan replied.

When the group went to the kitchen for water, Luca came over to them and took Phil aside. "I wanted to know if you could take me to the beach," Luca said. "I think we both could use an escape from here."

"Okay, let me just ask Muggsy if it's okay."

"She said it's okay. She is the one that told me to ask you."

Phil went to Muggsy's office and got the keys to the Hummer. They were soon pulling out of the driveway and speeding down the street.

"Why do you want to go to the beach?" Phil asked.

"I think it would help me relax," Luca replied.

An hour later, they got to Jones Beach. The air was filled with the soothing scent of the ocean. They ran and did some yoga, and they even meditated a bit. It was indeed a relaxing escape.

Later that night, while everyone else in the orphanage was sleeping, Phil woke up in the middle of the night to get a drink of water. Everything around him seemed fuzzy and weird. He began to walk down the stairs, and suddenly they disappeared and he was falling. It felt as if it were an endless drop, but finally he landed … hard. Piles of skeletons surrounded him, and worms were crawling through the eye sockets of the skulls. An oversized Azazelbog lifted him up by the neck. Azazelbog was five times his size, and he started playing with Phil as if he were a marionette.

Muggsy and the kids from the orphanage were standing lined up in front of them. Azazelbog picked Muggsy up and started feeding on her, and zombies crept out of the shadows and fed on the kids. Phil tried fighting the zombies off, but they kept grabbing at him …

Right at that moment, Phil woke up in a cold sweat. He struggled to go back to sleep but finally managed to.

The following day, he quickly got ready, trying not to draw too much attention to himself. He went down to the dining room, said hello to Doris, got a plate of fried eggs, and found a seat. As he ate, he thought about the dream he'd had. Was it just a dream or was it a vision? And would all life on earth be destroyed by Azazelbog's hand and the power of evil?

Calista, Lisa, and Madison came over and sat next to him. Calista kissed Phil, and the four of them began talking. When they were done eating breakfast, they went to the den and hung out. A little later, Lisa and Madison left the den, leaving Calista and Phil alone. He told her about the dream he had, and she was stunned.

"Oh my gosh, do you think it was a vision or just a dream?" Calista asked.

"I was asking myself the same question, but I don't know," Phil replied.

"You have to tell Muggsy about it," Calista said.

"I was thinking the same thing. Is she in her office?"

"Yes, I think so. Do you want me to come with you?"

"I think I should do this by myself," Phil said.

Phil went to Muggsy's office. "I have to talk to you about a dream I had," Phil told her. After he filled her in, he asked, "What do you think it was?"

"I'm not sure. Maybe it was just a dream, but we'll ask Ruth," Muggsy answered.

Muggsy made a quick call, and it wasn't long before the lift rose and Ruth and Gina walked out.

"You wanted to talk to me?" Ruth asked.

Phil and Muggsy told Ruth about the dream.

"So what do you think it was?" Phil asked.

"Well, it sounds like it was a *predictionality*. That is a dream that is a vision of events to come," Ruth explained.

"Can you change the future that is shown in the predictionality?" Phil asked.

"Yes, it is possible," Ruth replied.

"But it is very dangerous to change it," Gina added.

"How is it dangerous?" Muggsy asked.

Ruth and Gina were clearly hesitant to say anything. Muggsy darted her eyes between Gina and Ruth. They both knew that Muggsy would think they were trying to keep something from

Quest Inc. Muggsy was still staring at them when Ruth decided to explain.

"Well, when I was younger, there was a coven leader called Sir Gribben. He had a predictionality of the king of that time getting murdered. He tried to warn the king, but the king just thought that Sir Gribben was crazy. The king had Sir Gribben put to death by hanging."

"What happened to the king?" Phil asked.

"He was murdered a couple of days later, in just the way the predictionality had indicated," Ruth explained quietly, "You see, Phil, people are scared of what they do not understand, and people destroy what they are scared of."

They talked for a little longer, and soon after Phil left the office, he found Lisa watching TV in the game room. Phil walked into the room and sat next to her. They talked a little as the afternoon sluggishly crept on, turning hotter, almost sweltering. All of a sudden, the central air conditioner turned on and a crisp cool breeze swept through the orphanage.

The next morning after breakfast, Phil spent the morning outside with the girls. The clouds turned gray, and thunder abruptly ripped through the sky, so everybody went back inside. Stanchie and Melissa joined Phil, Lisa, and Calista in the den. Muggsy came into the room and told them that she had to speak to them. They went to the Quest Inc. headquarters and sat down.

Just then, they heard a strange sound. All of a sudden, Azazelbog appeared in the room, Becky in tow. Muggsy's eyes darted toward Becky with a surprised look.

"As I told you before, you fleshlings will never win this fight," Azazelbog hissed. "I will kill each and every one of you until Quest Inc. is destroyed."

Azazelbog waved his arms in the air, and they flew back, hitting the wall. He glided over to Stanchie and Melissa, pinning them to the ground. Azazelbog stared deep into Melissa's and Stanchie's eyes. The girls began to shake violently and scream in agony. Seconds later, they started to smoke. They yelled even louder in pain as flames engulfed them. Azazelbog smirked at them, and he and Becky disappeared.

Muggsy ran into the hall toward the lift, where she dropped to her knees and began to cry, and then she slowly crept back to the headquarters. They all looked down at the charred remains of Stanchie and Melissa. Lynda and Pat came over later to try to console everyone, but they only ended up crying themselves. Muggsy made arrangements for Stanchie and Melissa's funeral.

In the morning, everybody dressed in black and went to the wake. When they got to the funeral home, the funeral director was setting everything up for the funeral the next day. A little while later Zack, Matt, and Mr. and Mrs. Matthews came, and there was not a dry eye in the place. During the day, more and more people came and viewed the closed caskets. At the end of the day, seventy-five people had signed the funeral home guest book, and everybody finally left, leaving Muggsy and the kids alone.

The next morning at breakfast, they all were dressed in black. When Toby arrived, they headed to the chapel. More and more people gradually arrived; the seats were soon full and the chapel was packed.

People began walking up to the podium and giving speeches. Sometime later, they all began praying. When the service was over, Muggsy, Toby, and the funeral home directors carried the coffins out. They gently placed the two coffins into the hearse, and the mourners got into their vehicles and followed. When they got to Flushing Cemetery, they carried the coffins over to the two freshly dug graves.

They began praying again as they slowly lowed the coffins into the holes, and everybody started crying again. At one point, Muggsy thought she heard something, so she turned around. She looked over at a group of trees with a strange expression on her face

"Hey, Muggsy, what are you looking at?" Lynda asked.

"I just thought I heard something, and I thought I saw Becky," Muggsy said, "but I guess it was the wind blowing through the trees."

Everybody began dropping roses and handfuls of dirt into the holes. After some time, the cemetery workers took shovels and began covering the coffins with dirt. Gradually, everyone left, leaving Muggsy, Toby, and the kids alone to cry.

When they returned to the orphanage, Toby walked them inside. He and Muggsy went to her office. After a while, he emerged, said good-bye to everyone, and left the orphanage. It was nine o'clock by the time they ate dinner.

Over the next couple of days, the atmosphere was sad and quiet in the orphanage. It was the beginning of the week, on a Tuesday, when the mood eased slightly and everyone started talking and hanging out again.

Later that afternoon, Muggsy went to the boys' dorm and talked with Phil, who preferred to be alone. As the day dragged on, Phil remained in the dorm alone, although boys entered and exited the room the entire time.

After dinner, Phil was passing through the hallway when he found Muggsy in her office crying at her desk. "Are you okay?" he asked.

"I'm fine," Muggsy replied as she wiped the tears from her face. "I just miss Stanchie and Melissa."

"I miss them too."

"I can't believe that Becky went over to Azazelbog's side."

Muggsy frowned and punched the desk. The desk shook, and pencils leaped up and fell to the floor. "Suit up, Phil," she ordered. "The two of us and some Q.I. members are going to Flushing Cemetery and ending this crap."

He was more than happy to oblige, and he ran to the boys' dorm and quickly changed into his Q.I. suit. He returned to Muggsy's office, and they went to the living room. Lisa, Calista, Isaiah, and Brandon came a few minutes later, and they all piled into the Hummer. They pulled out of the driveway and sped down the street in the direction of the cemetery.

They all unloaded the mini stake cannons, loaded them with silver stakes, and entered the cemetery. A heavy thick fog covered the ground of the cemetery. They moved slowly, keeping on their guard so none of Azazelbog's goons would jump them.

It was strangely quiet and eerie knowing that Azazelbog and his followers were around. They all split up, taking different sections looking for them. A half hour later, they met back in the middle of the cemetery.

"Have you found anything?" Muggsy asked the boys.

"No, we didn't," one of them answered.

A minute later, Lisa and Calista came running. "There's no activity in the old run-down house," Lisa said.

"They must have known we were coming," Phil said.

Muggsy dropped to her knees with her arms raised into the air and screamed.

"Come on. We'd better go before Doris and the others start worrying," Phil suggested.

They helped Muggsy to her feet and quickly left.

The following morning after breakfast, Phil went outside to shoot some hoops, Isaiah and Brandon joining him. At eleven o'clock, Muggsy came outside and called them in for a Q.I. meeting. They all went into the house and down to headquarters. The meeting lasted twenty minutes.

Phil and Isaiah stopped Matt and Zack and asked how they were doing, and they both replied that they were doing a little better. They headed outside to hang out, and a few minutes later, Brandon joined them. They sat around on lawn chairs and just looked up at the sky.

Later that day, they decided to go skateboarding at the park. After doing some shredding, they played handball. At six o'clock, the boys went back to the orphanage. When they got back, they found Lisa, Madison, and Calista in the game room watching TV. Muggsy stuck her head into the room and called them down for dinner. When they got to the dining room, Phil helped himself to a veggie burger and french fries. The others sat down next to him, and they ate and talked. A half hour later, they took their dishes to the kitchen.

Matt's cell phone rang; he quickly answered it and talked to his mom. Two minutes later, he ended the call and put his phone back into his pocket. They went to Muggsy's office, and Phil told her that he was going to walk Matt and Zack home. They left the orphanage and skated down the street. When they got to Zack and Mat's house, Mrs. Matthews thanked Phil.

CHAPTER 12

The Preparations

When he was done eating the next morning, Phil went to Muggsy's office. She asked him to go pick up Zack and Matt. He grabbed his deck and left the house, and when he got outside, he hopped on his skateboard and began skating.

Ten minutes later, he was walking up the stoop to his friends' home. He, Zack, and Matt were soon heading to the orphanage.

"Why does Muggsy want to see us?" Zack asked.

"I think she wants you to try on your new techno-organic Q.I. Suits," Phil replied.

When they got to the orphanage, they went to Muggsy's office. "Hi, boys. How are you two doing?" Muggsy asked.

"We're doing better," Zack answered. "How are you feeling?"

"The same, I guess," Muggsy said.

Muggsy punched in the code, and the rickety lift slowly came clanging up. They quickly got on, and it descended again. When they got into headquarters, Ryan and Luca were waiting for them.

"Hi, Matt and Zack," Luca said. "I haven't seen you in a while."

"It's good to see you." Then they both turned around and gave Ryan a pound.

"We haven't seen you in a while," Matt said. "How's it hanging?"

"I'm chilling. We've been really busy here," Ryan replied.

"Here are your techno-organic Q.I. suits. We want to see how they fit you," Luca said, handing them two suits.

They took the suits and walked to the other side of headquarters. They returned moments later, wearing the suits. Suddenly, Ruth came into the room and whispered something in Muggsy's ears.

"Don't worry. I'll take care of it later," Muggsy said to Ruth.

"Now we want to test the techno-organic transformation," Luca said. "Think of any animal and the suit should change into that animal."

Matt thought of a gorilla and Zack thought of a cougar, and their suits slowly changed into a techno-organic looking gorilla and cougar humanoid.

"I feel such power," Matt grunted.

"I do too," Zack purred.

"The transformations last an hour and a half, so you will not be able to come out of the suit until that time is over," Ryan said.

They began testing the strength and the agility of the suits. An hour and a half later, the techno-organic humanoids slowly changed back into the regular techno-organic Q.I. suits. When they went back to the office, Luca and Ryan left, leaving Matt, Muggsy, Phil, and Zack alone. The four of them went to the dining room and chatted, Doris joining them as well.

Just then, they heard a loud noise coming from the hallway. Becky ran into the dining room breathlessly. Muggsy stared at Becky with a deadly look in her eyes. "How dare you show herself after betraying Quest Inc. and me!" Muggsy's eyes continued to shoot daggers at Becky, and she lunged forward at her. Ruth stepped in front of Muggsy to stop her.

"Think about what you are doing!" Ruth exclaimed.

"She helped Azazelbog kill my girls!" Muggsy screamed.

"Please calm down. Let me explain something to you," Ruth said.

"What do you mean by that?" Muggsy asked.

"I told Becky to go to Azazelbog and be a double agent for Quest Inc.," Ruth said.

Muggsy grabbed Ruth by the shoulders and frowned. "You mean this is your fault!" Muggsy exclaimed.

"Look, she was just supposed to go in, get information, and get right out," Ruth said. "No one was supposed to get killed."

"Yeah, but two people did die!" Muggsy exclaimed.

"And I'm very sorry that Stanchie and Melissa died," Becky said.

"Sorry doesn't mean anything to me," Muggsy said angrily. "And he could've read your mind, so why didn't Azazelbog know you were a double agent?"

"Because I placed an anti-detection spell on Becky," Ruth said.

And at that, tears rolled down Muggsy's face. She took a napkin and wiped them away.

Becky explained what Azazelbog had told her.

Muggsy took Ruth by the arm. "You are very close to being kicked out of Quest Inc.," Muggsy snapped.

Ruth and Becky left the dining room, leaving the others drowning in sadness and anger.

As the day sluggishly passed, the tension between Muggsy, Becky, and Ruth weighed heavily in the orphanage. It was early evening when Zack and Matt went home. After dinner, Zoe, Gina, and Becky went to their homes, and the others went to sleep. Phil spent half the night tossing and turning, unable to sleep.

The next morning, there was a lot of activity going on with the members of Quest Inc. Muggsy radioed Phil, Isaiah, Brandon, and Madison to come down to H.Q. When they got there, Muggsy sat them down and began talking.

"Our information shows that there will be a total eclipse in two weeks, and with the information that Becky gave us, there is a good chance that Azazelbog will try to take over then," Muggsy started to explain. "We are going to ask the Warriors of Raw for their help in this fight."

"So we are going to get to see our parents again," Madison and Isaiah said at the same time.

"We're getting prepared to contact them," Muggsy said, "so wait around and you can tell them."

Ryan set up the radio. "Okay, it's ready," he called out.

They went over to Ryan; Isaiah picked up the radio headset and turned it on. "Check one, two. Check one, two. Can anyone hear me? This is Isaiah. Is anyone there?"

For a second, there was very loud static, and then it went silent.

"I guess nobody's there. Don't worry—we'll try later," Muggsy said.

They all left, leaving Muggsy and Ryan alone. When they got upstairs, they went outside and sat talking. After some time, Isaiah, Madison, and Brandon went back inside. A little while later Phil, Lisa, and Calista went inside and headed to the den.

When the doorbell rang a short while later, Phil answered it. The postal carrier handed him a package and the mail. He went to Muggsy's office, placed the package and mail on the desk, and returned to the den for a while. He then went to the boys' dorm, turned on the computer, and used the Internet.

He was lying on his bed reading when Muggsy called him a bit later. After dinner, Phil went back up to the dorm and began reading again. Isaiah, Brandon, and Madison came into the dorm, and the four of them began to talk.

"Guess what," Isaiah said.

"What happened?" Phil asked.

"We radioed our parents, and they told Muggsy that they are going to help us in the fight," Brandon explained. "They will be arriving in two days' time."

"That's great news," Phil said.

Just then the others came into the room. Muggsy was close behind them, and before quickly leaving again, she told them that it was time for bed. Calista kissed Phil on the cheek, and she, Lisa, and Madison said good night to the other boys and left.

The next morning, after another restless night of sleep, Phil ate his breakfast, grabbed his skateboard, and left the orphanage; he skated down the walkway and out of sight. He slowly made his way to the library, and when he got there, he went to the religion, history, and microbiology sections.

A couple of hours later, he checked out a few books and left the library. On his way home, he stopped at Joe's Pizzeria and got a slice of pizza. When he got back home, he went straight to the boys' dorm, put his skateboard away, and began reading. After some time, he felt quite tired. He lay down and quickly passed out. Hours later, Phil woke up and yawned loudly. He looked at the clock and saw that it was eight o'clock.

He slowly got up from his bed and went down to the dining room. The room was empty and quiet, and there was a plate on the table, a folded piece of paper next to it. He unfolded the paper and read it:

Dear Phil,

Today is movie night so we all went to Fresh Meadows Movie Theater. I know how you like movie night, but I also knew you were tired and I didn't want to wake you. Oh, and I really have to talk to you when I come home. Enjoy dinner.

Love,
Muggsy

Phil threw away the note and ate his dinner. Then he went to the game room and watched TV. When the others came back, Muggsy took Phil to her office to talk to him.

The next morning Phil woke up and ate before hurrying to the den. He wanted to be left alone. He felt that if he was alone in silence, then none of his problems or thoughts could hurt him.

Suddenly, a strange feeling swept over his whole body; it was as if he were blanketed in bliss. A little while later, someone tapped him on the shoulder and he was kicked back into reality.

"Muggsy wants to see you," a boy said.

"Okay, thanks, bro," Phil answered.

They both left the den, and Phil headed to the office. "The Warriors of Raw are supposed to be arriving today, and I wanted you to help welcome them," Muggsy said.

"Okay, when are they getting here?" Phil asked.

"They'll be here in a half hour. Isaiah, Brandon, and Madison are already down in headquarters."

The two of them went down to join the others. A few moments later, Ryan walked over to Muggsy.

"There are going to be more people coming here along with the Warriors of Raw," Ryan said.

"What do you mean by that?" Muggsy asked.

"Well, Isaiah's mother said that Lord Devon wants to help in the fight," Ryan replied.

"Does he know what he's getting himself into? And is he ready for this battle?" Muggsy asked.

"Well, he did help fight those demons, and Ruth says he has some wicked awesome fighting skills."

"We really can't trust Ruth at this point after everything that went down," Muggsy answered.

"Listen, Muggsy, you're the only one who is still on that. Please let it go. And think of this: Becky could've died getting information for Quest Inc." And with that, Ryan strolled back over to the portal.

"Okay, it's all ready," Ryan called out a while later.

Ryan pressed a button, and lights turned on. The portal roared to life, and smoke bellowed from it. The prongs unlatched and fell to the floor, and the edge of the portal began to slowly turn. The solid center slowly dissolved, turning into the jellied center. A heavy gust of wind blew, blowing papers to the floor. The jelly center started to bubble, and a single hand came out, followed by the rest of Liza, Joseph, Anna, Lord Devon, and a small group of his guards. A couple of seconds later, a group of twenty men and women that Phil had never seen began coming through the portal.

"It's nice to see you again," Muggsy said.

"Who are they?" Phil asked.

"They are the Warrior Monks," Devon answered.

"Who are the Warrior Monks?" Phil asked.

"They are a group of monks from Old York New that had a vision to fight in this war," Lord Devon said. "They have been trained in every sort of combat possible."

"Are you sure they understand what they're getting into?" Muggsy asked. "Some of us might not make it out of this alive."

"We all understand what we are getting into," Lord Devon quickly said. "And we all said our good-byes to our loved ones."

They made their way up to the office. "We really don't have enough room for all of you to stay, so I'll ask a friend if some of you can stay with him," Muggsy said.

After a quick call, Muggsy got off the phone and looked over at the Warriors of Raw and Lord Devon. "Toby said some of you can stay with him." Muggsy began to say "So Devon and his guards and the Warrior Monks will stay with him."

Muggsy and the kids showed them around, and a half hour later, they ended up in the dining room.

"Go get your parents settled in," Muggsy said.

"We would love to," Madison said.

Ruth and the coven came to the orphanage, and Ruth introduced the coven to Lord Devon and the Warriors and Raw. Toby showed up next, and at seven o'clock, Doris everybody for dinner. When they were done eating, Toby, Lord Devon, his guards and the Warrior Monks left.

CHAPTER 13

The Apocalyptic War

The summer was nearing the end, and there was only a week and a half until school began. It all started the beginning of the week. The strong blinding light of the sun awoke everyone in the orphanage. Everybody got up and began getting ready; Phil was the only one still in bed. Muggsy came into the room and woke Phil up. After Phil had eaten breakfast, he went to the living room and turned on the TV.

A breaking news report came on and a news reporter started to talk. The reporter indicated that a total eclipse was going to start any second now, and the cameras pointed to the sky. Phil quickly ran outside to the front yard. Some of the neighbors were also outside waiting to see the eclipse. A few minutes later, the moon inched closer and closer to the sun, eventually covering it and making the whole sky dark. Phil noticed that the moon, sun, and the other planets began to align with the earth. All of a sudden, a huge gust of wind blew through the air and the earth began to quake.

Azazelbog suddenly appeared in Manhattan in front of the Empire State Building with his followers. *This will do just fine*, Azazelbog thought. He raised his arms and began chanting, and the ground started shaking hard. People started screaming and running. Lava oozed out of the streets around the Empire State Building, melting everything. Lava shot out of the street, engulfing the entire Empire State Building.

A few minutes later, the lava hardened to form a hard stone skin all around the building. Every inch of the newly coated Empire State Building had jagged edges in it, and there were small holes in the stone for windows. It looked like a demonic hellish castle. The people on the surrounding streets stared and pointed in fear of what had just happened. Suddenly, a large hole appeared in the side of the building. Azazelbog and his followers walked inside the building, and the hole sealed itself behind them.

Back at the orphanage, Phil was again watching TV when another special breaking news report came on. The news reporter announced what had happened to the Empire State Building. Phil's mouth dropped down in fear and shock, and he ran to Muggsy's office.

"You'd better take a look at this!" Phil exclaimed.

They ran to the living room, and Muggsy had the same look on her face that Phil had. The news cameras pointed to the Empire State Building, and the reporter began explaining what had happened.

"I didn't think this would happen right now," Muggsy said as she looked up at Phil. "Go tell everybody to suit up. We're going to Manhattan."

Phil went up to the dorms and told all the members of Quest Inc. to meet Muggsy in headquarters. Then he met Muggsy in the living room, and they both went down to headquarters. Ten minutes later, the lift opened again; Lynda, Pat, their husbands, and Pat's daughters came into the headquarters.

"Are you sure that Azazelbog is going to try to take over today?" Lynda asked.

"Well, I'm pretty sure. All the signs that Becky told us about are happening now," Muggsy said. "And Azazelbog told Becky that he will be at full strength when all these signs occur."

When Toby, Ruth, the other Q.I. Members, and the coven arrived, Muggsy said, "Everyone please suit up in your new techno-organic suits and grab a mini stake cannon, exploding sprout, and vegetating humanoid. Then meet me back here."

Just as Toby was going to go change into his Q.I. suit Muggsy stopped him. "Where are the Guardians of Souls and the Warriors of Raw?" she asked.

"They're upstairs putting their armor on," Toby replied.

"And where are Devon, his guards, and the Warrior Monks?" Muggsy asked.

"They're also upstairs getting ready," Toby answered.

Muggsy and Toby went and changed into the Q.I. suits. Ten minutes later, everyone came back with the suits on. Everyone went back up in two groups and met the others in the living room.

Pat turned around and looked at her daughters, and tears began rolling down her cheeks. Both of her daughters wiped the tears from Pat's face.

"Are you okay, Mom?" one of her daughters asked. "What happened?"

"I don't want you two to fight in this battle," Pat said.

"We're part of Quest Inc., so this is our fight, too," her other daughter said. "We are ready for this fight and for all the consequences."

"Your dad gave me the same answer," Pat said. "The both of you are as stubborn as your father." They smiled and hugged each other.

A few minutes later, Muggsy started to speak. "I just wanted to say that we're not only fighting this battle for Quest Inc. We're fighting for all humankind."

Muggsy pulled Toby aside. "Is anyone else helping us with this battle? We only have a handful of people, and I'm scared we won't win this fight."

"Don't worry—Quest Inc.'s international operatives are going to come and fight by our side."

Ryan came out of the office wearing a Q.I. suit.

"I thought you said you didn't like fighting," Muggsy said.

"Usually I'm a lover not a fighter, but I feel I have to fight in this battle," Ryan answered.

"Ruth, please come over here," Muggsy called out.

Ruth did as she asked.

"Do you remember the driving lessons I gave you?" Muggsy asked.

"Yes, I do," Ruth replied.

"Good. I want you to drive the Hummer." Muggsy handed Ruth the keys. "Oh, and I'm sorry for giving you such a hard time."

"Do not worry about it," Ruth said.

"Phil, do you have the Dagger of Destiny?" Muggsy asked.

"Yes," Phil answered.

"Okay, everybody, let's go," Muggsy said.

Everyone grabbed weapons and ran out of the orphanage, and Muggsy closed the door behind her. They all got into the Hummer, Range Rover, and a long white van. Toby, Ruth, and Muggsy got into the drivers' seats, and seconds later, the vehicles sped away.

In Manhattan, the ground started to shake around the hellish Empire State Building, and lava shot out of the ground. Seconds later, writhing demons and two dragons climbed out of the huge crack. The demons held on to the dragons' razor-sharp talons, and they flew into the air. Storm clouds started rolling in, and lightning and claps of thunder ripped through the afternoon sky. The dragons landed on top of the suspension cables of the Brooklyn Bridge. The demons jumped down onto the bridge and began howling and beating their chests.

The people got out of their vehicles and ran up the bridge, screaming and crying for their lives. The dragons began writhing and roaring spitting fire into the air and down at the bridge. Both dragons flew down onto the bridge, and the dragons and demons started devouring the people, agonizing bloodcurdling screams filling the air. With every step the creatures took, the bridge began to crack. A couple of minutes later, the Brooklyn Bridge started to crumble. It wasn't long before it collapsed into the river. The demons grabbed on to the dragons' talons again, and they flew to Azazelbog's new castle.

Inside the hellish castle, nothing resembled the Empire State Building. Everything was surrounded by hardened lava, and tiny flames danced around the whole place. Azazelbog's throne room looked like a huge flame made out of hardened lava. Azazelbog sat on his throne; he lifted both arms and began chanting. Electricity started hitting the throne, and a golden-black aura formed around Azazelbog's entire body. An evil grin swept over his face.

"I feel all my power coming back to me," Azazelbog wailed happily. "And it feels good."

His returning power pulsed through his body as the golden-black aura grew stronger and stronger. Azazelbog's demon form tried to break out of Alex's body, but he stopped it from happening. After some time, two of Azazelbog's followers brought him a young plump man who was shackled.

"Oh, my lunch."

"Please don't do anything to me," the man begged.

"Shut up, you fat fleshling. I'm getting tired of your begging, and it will not get you anywhere."

Azazelbog opened his mouth wide and devoured the man whole.

Quest Inc.'s vehicles were just entering the city. They had noticed that groups of about a dozen or so people, young and old, were trying to leave the city. They saw fires engulfing a few of the buildings and huge plumes of smoke billowing out of other buildings. Phil looked up out of the Hummer window and saw the dragons flying overhead in the sky. The dragons were spitting out big balls of fire in all directions.

He looked back at the streets and saw wounded people lying in the streets crying in agony for help. Two large demons were throwing a man back and forth to each other as if he were a basketball.

Four army choppers appeared in the air. When the choppers landed, the people in Q.I. suits jumped down from the choppers and ran and greeted them.

"We have to get all these people out of Manhattan and the wounded some medical attention," Phil said.

Just then, an enormous group of men and women walked up to them.

"These are the many covens in New York," Ruth began to explain. "They want to help in this battle."

"Okay, we need all the help we can get!" Muggsy exclaimed. "Load them up with the techno-organic weapons."

Ryan, Ruth, and Luca handed the newcomers the techno-organic weapons. Some of the others picked up the wounded and led them out of the city.

The demons saw the Quest Inc. members and started fighting them. Phil and Muggsy took their mini stake cannons and shot silver stakes at some demons. One of the demons pulled the stake out of his chest and threw it onto the ground; the flesh wound sizzled as the demon screamed in agony. Ruth, Gina, and some members of other covens started chanting spells. Demons flew into building walls and fell to the ground with loud thuds.

Huge pieces of the buildings crumbled, falling on top of the demons. A large hole appeared at the top of the hellish castle, and Azazelbog glided out and stood there with an evil grin on his face and his eyes glowing bright yellow.

"I'm tired of playing games with you, filthy fleshling," Azazelbog hissed loudly. "You think you can fight me? I will give you something to fight. "To my unruly warriors and soldiers, arise and vanquish these fleshling vermin!"

The ground quaked, and the streets started to crack and crumble, and out of the ground rose thousands of graves. The graves opened, and zombies slowly climbed out of them. A grin came across Azazelbog's face, and the Deval demon ran out of the castle and jumped down, landing on its feet on the street below. Azazelbog went back inside, and the hole sealed up behind him. Moments later, everyone started to fight. Spells were being cast in all directions, and demons were tossed into the air and thrown back down.

Phil, Ryan, and some other Quest Inc. members threw a couple of exploding sprouts toward the demons, and they exploded. Roots quickly grew, grabbing hold of the demons and twisting them and ripping them apart. The zombies began biting people, and demons picked up other people and threw them into the walls of buildings. A dozen vegetating humanoids explosives were thrown. They exploded, and the humanoids jumped down and began fighting.

The battle went on for hours, and there were bodies of humans and demons cascading all over the streets. More and more demons came out from under the ground and began fighting. More exploding sprouts and vegetating humanoid grenades were thrown into the air. The covens cast spells banishing demons, and zombies back to hell. A wave of the techno-organic suits changed into techno-organic animals, and they fought.

A group of a dozen Q.I. members surrounded the hellish castle. Some time had passed and Lynda and Jay found an entrance hole in the corner. The group entered the castle. Minutes passed with nobody coming back out. Phil was getting worried and could not concentrate on the fight. Bad thought were running through his head. He began to run, slicing the demons with his sword, making his way over to Muggsy.

"Lynda, Jay, and some other Q.I. members went into the castle and haven't come out yet," Phil said.

"That's strange. I'm worried also," Muggsy said. "But we can help them."

"How? The hole they entered through sealed up, and that was the only one," Phil said.

"I have an idea. We're going to make our own entrance. Follow me," Muggsy said.

They got into the Hummer, and Muggsy started the ignition. She backed the Hummer up and sped forward. They sped faster and faster and then jumped a steep ramp and flew through the air. The Hummer broke through the castle wall, landing on one of the middle floors, and they got out.

"What now?" Phil asked.

"We search for Azazelbog and the others," Muggsy said.

A dragon snatched suddenly both of them and carried them away. The dragon grunted as it climbed higher and higher. The dragon eventually dropped them into a hallway and flew out of sight. Phil and Muggsy walked down the hallway with the mini stake cannons at the ready, in case something attacked them. The hallway led them to two large doors. On the doors was a large engraving of a pentagram, an outline of a demon in it.

The two doors opened by themselves, and Phil and Muggsy walked inside. The doors led them to the throne room. Lynda, Jay, and the other Q.I. members were shackled to a wall. A demon was clawing at two people; Phil took his cannons and shot stakes at the demon.

Muggsy and Phil picked the locks and unshackled them. Azazelbog glided over to Muggsy and Phil and slapped the stake cannons out of their hands. He circled around and landed right in front of them. He started to growl and grunt, and once again, Azazelbog's demon form tried to escape, but he stopped it again.

"See, Muggsy, he can't even control himself," Phil shouted, trying to anger him.

"Don't worry; you stupid fleshlings will not live to see next week," Azazelbog hissed. "Do you want me to divulge to you why Gittman and Keals were evil? They both sold their souls to my father and me." Azazelbog had a grin on his face. "They summoned us on their deathbeds and begged us for more time to live, and that is when they gave up their souls to us, turning them evil."

"I could believe that!" Phil exclaimed.

"But your parents and grandparents were too good for that," sneered Azazelbog.

Phil drew his sword, and Azazelbog's nails grew sharper and doubled their usual size, now resembling swords. As they began fighting, each slash that Phil's sword made into the nails of Azazelbog made clanging sounds. Suddenly, Azazelbog glided over to one of the Q.I. members and slashed him in the stomach and legs. The boy fell down legless into a pool of his own blood. Azazelbog turned around, grinning at Phil. Phil ran toward him and plunged his sword into Azazelbog's chest; he grabbed Phil and threw him to the ground. Azazelbog slowly pulled the sword out, glaring at the blood.

"You fleshlings will not win this war," he stated.

Azazelbog threw the sword at him, and Phil quickly jumped out of the way. Phil jumped into the air and karate kicked Azazelbog in the face. Muggsy shot a silver stake at Azazelbog; he snatched the stake and threw it at Muggsy, piercing her leg. She screamed in pain and fell to the ground.

Phil ran over to Muggsy and knelt down. "Are you okay?" Phil asked.

"Yes. It's just a flesh wound," Muggsy said.

"Okay, that's it! I'm getting tired of the crap!" Phil exclaimed.

He pressed the button on the suit, and the helmet latched on. He started thinking, and it slowly changed into a techno-organic cougar humanoid.

"Let's do this!" Phil roared.

The tail of the cougar wrapped itself around Azazelbog and threw him behind the throne. He got back up, spread his wings, and glided to Phil, punching him in the face. A couple of minutes later, a group of demons came into the throne room and began fighting the other Quest Inc. members. Phil grabbed Azazelbog by the neck, ran with him out to the balcony, and jumped off. Azazelbog fell to the ground with a loud earth-shattering thud. Phil slowly scaled down, and when he got halfway, he jumped the rest of the way to the street.

Phil made his way over to Azazelbog, thinking he was dead. After all, what could possibly survive such a long drop? However, Azazelbog's wings slowly moved, and a minute later, they started to flap. Azazelbog slowly rose up with his eyes closed; he snatched Phil, raising him into the air. He dropped Phil to the ground and picked him up again. Azazelbog threw Phil on the ground once more. Slowly Phil got back to his feet.

Phil looked around and saw zombies running around on fire, slowly turning into ashes. Others were being ripped apart by exploding sprouts and the vegetating humanoids. There were more zombies and demons, but the humans seemed to be winning the fight. At that very moment, more lava bellowed up from out of the ground and more demons flooded the streets. Now the demons and zombies had the upper hand. The many different covens were casting even more spells, and people were throwing exploding sprouts and vegetating humanoids.

Phil got back to his feet; he and Azazelbog started fighting again. Azazelbog took Phil by the neck and flew into the air with him again. He threw Phil hard to the ground. Phil's suit cracked, turning back into the regular techno-organic Q.I. suit. The helmet fell off and rolled to the far corner of the street.

Do you want me to introduce you to all the souls I have captured?" Azazelbog asked.

Phil stared at him with a confused look on his face. Large warts appeared on Azazelbog's face, and then faces formed on the warts. The faces began crying and screaming in tormented agony. Phil recognized one of the faces; it was the face of Alex.

"Please help me, Phil. Please help me," Alex's face cried out in agony.

Phil took out the Dagger of Destiny and tried to stab Azazelbog in the chest, but he grabbed the dagger and broke it in half, throwing it to the ground.

Azazelbog picked Phil up. "Did you really think a fleshling like you could kill me?" Azazelbog snarled. "Do you want to see what I truly look like?"

His eyes began glowing and his skin started peeling away. Azazelbog's true demon form appeared. He had a bony body and long razor-sharp nails. There was no nose, only bony hooked nostrils. Azazelbog's jaw appeared to be decaying, and his teeth were sharp and tiny like pine needles. When Phil looked around and saw a chapel, he remembered what the books from the library said.

"Everybody head to that chapel!" Phil called out.

He quickly picked up the two broken dagger pieces. All the humans ran into the chapel and barricaded the doors closed with benches.

"Why are we in here? We should be out there fighting," one of Pat's daughters said.

"First of all, evil can't enter a holy place," Phil said. "And second, we are getting whipped out there. We need to regroup and think of a new strategy so we can win this war."

Hearing the rustle of wings, they looked out the windows. The demon forces were flying all around the chapel. The candles blew out, and the light began flickering off and on. The door blew open, and splintered wood flew all over the place. Benches flew into the air and crashed down, breaking into pieces. Azazelbog and a small group of demons glided into the chapel. Azazelbog went over to Becky and grabbed her by the neck.

"I will take care of you later, filthy witch," he said. He threw her against a wall, and she fell to the ground.

Azazelbog went over to Phil and picked him up by the neck. "Did you forget that I can read your thoughts? The stupid fleshlings who wrote those books were wrong. They did not know the immense power of evil." Azazelbog ripped the techno-organic Q.I. suit off of Phil. "I want to see you before I kill you."

Zoe started chanting a binding spell, but when Azazelbog waved his left hand, Zoe's mouth suddenly vanished. Without Azazelbog noticing, Phil threw one of the dagger halves over to Muggsy, and she caught it. Azazelbog wrapped his long snakelike tongue around Phil's body.

"Now it is time for you to die, fleshlings," Azazelbog snapped.

"No, it's time for you to do the dying, asshole," Phil said.

"Asshole. I like that," Azazelbog said.

Phil took the broken half of the dagger and shoved it into Azazelbog's chest; Muggsy ran behind Azazelbog and shoved the other half of the dagger into his back. The two dagger halves connected inside his body, and a bright blinding light shined out of his body. Azazelbog cried and screamed in agony as an oozy, acidy blood poured out of the wound.

A couple of minutes later, the ground began to shake even harder than it had the previous times. The floor of the chapel began cracking, and a hole appeared. A huge demon rose out of the hole and moved over to them. It picked up Azazelbog, pulled the dagger out of his chest, and threw it on the ground. A single sizzling tear rolled off the demon's cheek and splashed onto the wound, and the demon stared at Azazelbog.

The demon wrapped its wings over Azazelbog, covering his entire body. Azazelbog snarled and whimpered in pain. Holding Azazelbog, the demon glided over to the members of Quest Inc. and started growling and snapping at them.

"Look what you did to my son!" the demon screamed. "That is right—I am Lucifer!"

The Quest Inc. members were horrified.

"Quest Inc. and you filthy fleshlings might have won this fight, but the war between good and evil will forever wage on," Lucifer hissed. "Quest Inc. will not always be around to help, and that is when you filthy infestation known as humanity will be extinguished."

Lucifer growled and snarled, and holding Azazelbog, he flew out of the chapel. The demons followed him.

The Quest Inc. members slowly followed the demons out of the chapel. Phil noticed that the zombie warriors had disappeared and the demons were following Lucifer and Azazelbog back into the crack near the hellish Empire State Building. The lava rose up again, plugging up the cracks, and moments later, the lava hardened.

Phil slowly placed the dagger and his sword into the scabbard. He looked up and saw a star shining brightly, and a shooting star shot right by it. Phil and Muggsy looked at each other and smiled.

Calista walked over to them and hugged Phil. "Do you think that Alex's soul is finally at peace now?" she asked.

"I think so, Calista. I really think so," Phil replied.

The hellish castle slowly began turning back into the regular Empire State Building. They all got back into the vehicles and drove away.

Epilogue

Seasons came and went, and years passed, yet the Glance of Angels Orphanage and Quest Inc. still stood strong. There was a new face at the desk where Muggsy had once worked. He was a gentleman with wavy blond hair. A wooden nameplate on the desk read PHILLIP R. Suddenly, a woman came into the office accompanied by a teenage boy. The women had long blonde hair, and she was tall. The boy had brown hair and blues eyes. He was skinny, and he was wearing a Quest Inc. suit.

"Dad, are you coming?" the boy asked.

"Yes, I am," Phil answered. "Is everybody ready?"

"The new recruits are headed to headquarters as we speak. Aunt Lisa, Madison, Uncle Brandon, and Isaiah are waiting in the living room," the boy said.

"Junior's just excited because he's going to be junior commander," Calista said.

A minute later, an older Muggsy walked into the office assisted by a cane. Muggsy looked the same but with gray hair.

"Of course Phil Junior is excited about being a junior commander," Muggsy said. "He's following in his father's footsteps."

"Let's head to H.Q. for the meeting," Phil said.

The three of them left what was now Phil's office and went to the living room. They found Lisa, Isaiah, Madison, and Brandon talking on the sofa. They left the living room and went to the garage, where Phil punched in a code. A portion of the wall detached and moved. They started their descent.

About the Book

After Phil returns home from college, he finds out that things have changed. Muggsy has gone back to old habits; and Isaiah, Brandon, and Madison are the new junior commanders of Quest Inc.

But when the son of the highest evil threatens Quest Inc. and the world, Phil must join Q.I. as head junior commander again. Can Phil and Quest Inc. retrieve the Spear of Destiny and save our world, or will demons cause our world to end?

About the Author

Lynn Mathai is a file clerk at a bank. When he is not working, he likes spending time with his family and friends. He also enjoys writing short stories for his niece and nephews.

CPSIA information can be obtained
at www.ICGtesting.com
Printed in the USA
FFOW02n1733130215
11100FF

9 781496 940322